HIDEOUT VALLEY

His name was Jim Bannister. He did not look like someone on the dodge, who had seen his way of life destroyed and himself hounded by all the power of a million dollar combine. And with a $12,000 reward for his capture, he always lived with the shadow of a rope upon him. For now under the assumed name of Jim Bryan he was temporary marshal in Morgan Valley, a town that he had felt easy in—until he found his own Wanted poster lying in full view on the floor of his office.

He braced himself for a showdown with his unknown enemy and waited . . .

D(wight) B(ennett) Newton is the author of a number of notable Western novels. Born in Kansas City, Missouri, Newton went on to complete work for a Master's degree in history at the University of Missouri. From the time he first discovered Max Brand in Street and Smith's *Western Story Magazine*, he knew he wanted to be an author of Western fiction. He began contributing Western stories and novelettes to the Red Circle group of Western pulp magazines published by Newsstand in the late 1930s. During the Second World War, Newton served in the US Army Engineers and fell in love with the central Oregon region when stationed there. He would later become a permanent resident of that state and Oregon frequently serves as the locale for many of his finest novels. As a client of the August Lenniger Literary Agency, Newton found that every time he switched publishers he was given a different byline by his agent. This complicated his visibility. Yet in notable novels from *Range Boss* (1949), the first original novel ever published in a modern paperback edition, through his impressive list of titles for the Double D series from Doubleday, *The Oregon Rifles, Crooked River Canyon,* and *Disaster Creek* among them, he produced a very special kind of Western story. What makes it so special is the combination of characters who seem real and about whom a reader comes to care a great deal and Newton's fundamental humanity, his realization early on (perhaps because of his study of history) that little that happened in the West was ever simple but rather made desperately complicated through the conjunction of numerous opposed forces working at cross purposes. Yet, through all of the turmoil on the frontier, a basic human decency did emerge. It was this which made the American frontier experience so profoundly unique and which produced many of the remarkable human beings to be found in the world of Newton's Western fiction.

HIDEOUT VALLEY

D. B. Newton

GUNSMOKE

This hardback edition 2008
by BBC Audiobooks Ltd
by arrangement with
Golden West Literary Agency

ISBN 978 1 405 68220 6

British Library Cataloguing in Publication Data available.

Printed and bound in Great Britain by
CPI Antony Rowe, Chippenham, Wiltshire

CHAPTER I

From the high window where Jim Bannister stood he had a view over almost all of Morgantown, crammed antigodlin fashion into the throat of its steep gulch with the snow-blocked hills behind. Pillars of chimney smoke rose in thin winter light. On the upper slopes a few slag heaps and abandoned mine buildings still showed that, while Morgan Valley might be cattle country now, the town had actually had its start as a gold camp.

Bannister was observing the progress of a bulky figure in a buffalo coat moving erratically along the street down there at the bottom of the gulch. Even from this foreshortened distance it was obvious the man carried too heavy a load of liquor. Bannister's impersonal gaze followed him across the muddy street ruts, watched him flounder through a knee-deep pile of dirty snow and finally achieve a stand on uneven sidewalk planking: the man braced himself there, leaning a hand against a porch prop and looking around uncertainly.

As he had done many times of late Bannister thought coldly, and without much real pity. I'd like to know where the devil *that's* going to end. Not in my lap, I hope. . . .

Aware then of a sudden quiet in the room, he turned. The poker players at the round mahogany table were looking directly at him; so was the woman who stood holding a silver tray containing a decanter and glasses.

She was coolly blond, smoothly and carefully groomed in a soft gray dress of some material that had not come from any of the dingy little stores in the gulch below. Bannister met her stare and mumbled belatedly, "Sorry, ma'am. Were you speaking to me?"

"I was indeed," she answered in a husky voice that fell oddly on a man's ears. "Would you like a drink, Mister Bryan?"

5

Bryan . . .

He drew in a shallow breath, hiding the brief stab of alarm. After so many months he should have grown accustomed enough to the name, not to let it pass over his head unheard and unanswered. It had been a bad slip and he felt the back of his neck grow warm. With all of them watching him he told the woman, "No drink, Mrs. Youngdahl. Thanks."

She could not have cared less. She placed the tray on the table beside her husband, who moved his arm slightly to make room. Then, her duties as hostess fulfilled, she returned to the high-backed chesterfield and the book she'd left by the blazing fieldstone fireplace.

Claude Youngdahl's sharp stare continued a moment longer to regard Bannister, expressionless above the fan of cards he held propped in front of his chest. The tall man had to steel himself to meet it, wondering what thought lay behind the eyes. But then Youngdahl dropped his glance to the cards, ran the ball of a thumb across their faces. He folded them, placed them in front of him, and deliberately counted out a stack of chips into the center of the table.

Feeling uncomfortable, and ignored, and a little angry, Jim Bannister waited for the hand to be played out.

Two of the players threw in their cards and, on the showdown, Youngdahl won. He made no move to haul in the pot. Letting the chips lie, he uncorked the decanter his wife had brought, poured himself two fingers of the amber whiskey and passed it on. Having taken a swallow, he turned at last directly to the tall man in the muddy boots and the unbuttoned Windbreaker and shapeless Stetson. He made a curt, summoning motion with his head that brought Jim Bannister forward. "Well, Bryan?" he said impatiently.

Bannister downed the sting of resentment, but his voice was sharp as he reminded the other, "You asked me up here—remember? You said the council had business with me."

"I suppose I did at that." The banker sounded as though it had slipped his mind. "Well, then—let's get on with it." He finished his drink, set the glass down.

6

Their attention was all on Jim Bannister, now—five men in shirtsleeves, coats hung on the backs of their chairs. They all had whiskey glasses in front of them, amid the litter of chips and cards; though, likely out of deference to the woman and to the wealth of the room's furnishings, no one was smoking.

These were the members of the city council—the important men of Morgantown. That they should all be inveterate card players, who mingled business with pleasure during their twice-weekly poker sessions, was more or less beside the point.

Joe Ries, the town's druggist, who was also mayor, should have been the one to conduct their meetings; but maybe Claude Youngdahl's bank was holding a note against his inventory. He made no objection as Youngdahl took charge, with characteristic bluntness: "Bryan, I'm afraid we're not too pleased with the setup down there in the town marshal's office."

"No?" Bannister said.

"It's a peculiar situation, you'll have to admit. How long is it you've been filling in while Sam White's laid up? Four months, at least."

Carefully he agreed. "Something like that."

"Well—whatever. It's been too long! The council has decided it wants a change."

"Your privilege," Bannister said roughly. "I've tried to do the job. If it hasn't been good enough, I'm sorry." He pushed aside the front of his Windbreaker, started to work at the fastening of the metal star pinned to his shirt. "I won't beg to go on wearing this."

"Oh, now, hold on!" That was Lloyd Canby, the general storekeeper—a middle-aged, soft, good-natured man whom Bannister had come to look on almost as a friend. "I think you misunderstand," he said hastily. "Nobody's criticizing you, Jim."

Puzzled, Bannister looked at him and dropped his hand again. "What, then?"

"Doc . . ." Youngdahl looked to the man seated next to him—a tidy little man with skin like parchment and a trim,

7

white goatee at the end of his long jaw. "Give us your professional opinion. Just what do you make of Sam White's condition?"

Henry Barnhouse scowled uncomfortably. "You shouldn't put me in this spot," he protested. "It ain't ethical—a doctor discussing his patient's condition. . . ."

"No matter," the banker said firmly. "You owe a responsibility to this council. We pay the man's salary. If he isn't up to earning it, we have every right to know."

"That's true, but—" Breaking off, Doc Barnhouse let his narrow shoulders lift in a sigh; he shook his head unhappily. "Well, no. I can't pretend I'm satisfied about Sam. The bullet hole in his leg appears completely healed, but that bout he had with pneumonia didn't help matters. It's cleared up now, of course. Still, coming on top of the other, it's sapped his strength and maybe even the will to get better. Sometimes," he pointed out, "when a man reaches a certain age—"

"Is it your opinion White's too old for his job?"

Reluctantly he admitted it. "I just don't know. I dunno what else would drain the strength and the spirit completely out of a man. . . ."

Youngdahl swung back to stab Bannister with keen black eyes. "There you have it," he said crisply. "This town needs a full-time marshal—not one man on the permanent sick list, and another filling his office for him from week to week without adequate pay or a guarantee of tenure."

"I've got no gripe," Bannister put in quickly.

"But *we* have! White's not only letting us down, but the county sheriff's office. I think you know the arrangement: It's been understood that whatever man we appoint as town marshal, draws extra money as the deputy for this Morgan Valley district. Between the two, the pay is well worth collecting. And right now Sam White's doing nothing to earn it.

"Perhaps this hasn't mattered too much, up to now," he conceded. "But one of these days the passes will be open again. By the time spring comes we're determined to have an effective law office functioning here. . . . What about it— would you be interested?"

8

Jim Bannister blinked, taken completely by surprise. "Do I understand you're talking about firing Sam, and offering me his place?"

The banker nodded. "Put briefly—that's it."

It was the last thing he had expected. Stalling, he asked, "And what does Sam say to this?"

"He's got nothing to say!" Claude Youngdahl snapped. "It's the council's decision."

"Meaning, you haven't even told him . . . ?"

"No."

Anger and indignation began to do their work. "Seems to me kind of a shabby way to treat a man, after five years—or however long it's been."

Youngdahl's head tilted sharply, his cheeks pinching and changing color; he stared at Bannister. It was Sid Noon, the livery stable owner with the craggy, battered face and the iron-gray shock of hair, who answered.

"Nobody asked your opinion," Noon retorted, leaning sharply forward in his chair. "The five of us have to think of what's best for the community. Now, the job's there; some of the council think you should be given first chance, if you want it. All we're asking from you is a straight yes or no!"

Jim Bannister let them wait while he considered this. It did not sound to him like Lloyd Canby, or the little doctor, though it would be easy enough to outvote the two of them if the rest had their minds made up. He had a strong feeling Claude Youngdahl's was the dominating voice, and he looked at the man thoughtfully.

There was something vaguely repellent about him—the smooth-cheeked face too pale, the clean-shaven lips too red and full and unpleasantly moist. He looked soft, but the black stare held a warning of the iron within.

How, at scarcely more than thirty, Claude Youngdahl had been able to build a banking practice and buy and restore this monster of a house that had belonged to a manager of the defunct Morgan Mine, was really something to ponder. Inherited wealth no doubt had something to do with it, but the shrewdness and business sense with which Youngdahl managed his affairs were entirely his own.

And the sleek blond woman, observantly watching from

9

the sofa yonder, was herself somehow a part of his display of power and affluence. She went with the polished furniture, the velvet window drapes, and deep-napped carpet and the jeweled studs gleaming in this prosperous young man's shirtfront. Irene Youngdahl seemed aware of her function and, so far as Bannister could tell, minded not at all.

Sid Noon prodded: "Well?"

He drew a breath, chose his words carefully. "I never thought, in wearing Sam White's badge, I was doing more than holding things down till he could take over again. The job itself doesn't impress me as being so tough."

"It's apt to get tougher," Lloyd Canby said. The storekeeper pushed a hand across his scalp, nervously smoothing flat the thinning strands of hair. "I think you all know what it is that troubles me. There's things afoot could tear this Morgan Valley to pieces, if something isn't done!"

Bannister found himself unable to answer that, because he saw the sense of it. Unbidden, the image of a man in a buffalo coat, aimlessly stumbling through drifts at the foot of the hill, flashed across his mind. But he said, "At the very most I planned on staying till the passes open—no longer than that. After all, I figure Sam did me a personal favor. If what you want is someone to push him out of his job, you're going to have to get yourselves another man. Me, I'll drift."

The black eyes in the banker's smooth face probed his for a long moment. Bannister read the look, and found real displeasure in it. This was not what Youngdahl had wanted; suddenly the thought occurred to him: There's more here than meets the eye. This man has some scheme or other up his sleeve—and I've crossed him up. . . .

Youngdahl said gruffly, "You speak plain enough!"

"I meant to. And so much for that. Did you have anything else in mind you wanted to see me about?"

"No." The banker gave a curt shake of the head. "I guess you can go along."

"All right."

"I'll see Mister Bryan to the door," the woman said unexpectedly.

There was no good reason why she should; nevertheless,

10

she had risen and was coming toward him, the material of the full skirt sliding along her thighs with each easy step. Youngdahl was already giving his full attention to gathering and stacking the chips from that last-won pot, while Joe Ries picked up the cards and began to shuffle.

Thus perfunctorily dismissed, Bannister shrugged and fell in beside his hostess. He had to bend his head slightly to clear the arch, as he went with her out into the front hallway.

Sid Noon had a voice that carried even when he imagined he was speaking softly. Hardly out of the room, Bannister clearly heard the liveryman's fierce half-whisper: "I still say we never did want him! Just who the hell *is* this Jim Bryan, anyway—if it's really his name, and for some reason I've got my doubts! What was Sam ever really able to tell us about him? Almost nothing! Damn it, I at least say, before we plan to pin the star on any man, permanent, we got a right to know who and what he—"

The last words were swallowed away, as though Noon had been warned to silence. Bannister and Irene Youngdahl were left in stillness beside the big front door with its mosaic of colored glass.

There was a hint of a smile at one corner of her mouth. "A man of mystery!" she said, the knowingness of her cool, blue-eyed regard faintly mocking him. "Did you realize that was what you'd made of yourself, Mister—Bryan?" The hesitation before the name didn't escape him.

He would not rise to the baiting. "No mystery about me, Mrs. Youngdahl."

"You really believe that?" She put out a hand, laid one finger on the sleeve of his rough and worn blanket coat. "Then it's only because you haven't been able to hear *all* the questions that have been asked behind your back, in this grubby little town, this past winter! There's nothing much for entertainment except gossip, in a place that's snow-bound four months out of the year. And there's been no better subject for tongue wagging lately, than you!"

Bannister frowned, and as he did he glimpsed their joint reflection in a heavy-framed mirror on the wall. The woman stood closer than she needed to, and her hand lay on his

11

sleeve in a manner that looked oddly like a caress. She appeared shapely and small indeed, beside this tall, rugged figure that topped nearly every other man he had ever met.

"Maybe you ought to tell your friends," he said gruffly, "they might do better to take up quilt-making or something." The amusement in her eyes seemed to deepen as he turned abruptly to open the big door, taking his arm from beneath her hand. "Afternoon, ma'am," he said.

Then he was outside on the veranda with the door closing and Morgantown lying in the iron grip of winter, spread below his feet. He drew a deep breath of icy air that dried out his nostrils, and pulled on his sweat-stained hat.

So, Morgantown was asking questions. . . . *Just who the hell is this Jim Bryan?* He could almost hear the echo of Noon's rasping voice. *If that's really his name . . .*

Lifting his head, he looked for a moment toward the mountains that walled in this remote corner of the world. Their tops were lost in the cloud ceiling; but though the passes were still closed he had been told that, in a case of necessity, a man on webs or horseback who did not mind the risk of being engulfed by unexpected slides of rotten snow could probably beat his way through. He was almost tempted.

But it would be a poor sort of thanks to Sam White, at a moment when his enemies on the council seemed determined to have the old man's scalp. Jim Bannister regretfully shrugged the thought away, and settled his hat more firmly. He was fastening the catches of his Windbreaker as he started down into the town.

CHAPTER II

Wood smoke, lacing the chill winter's breath, reminded Bannister that he should see to replenishing the fuel supply for the marshal's office. He had spoken about this to Bert

Dakins, the jailer, but had found it never paid to depend too much on Dakins.

The low cloud ceiling that strained out the fading light of afternoon looked as though it could be ready to drop more snow on this Colorado high country—perhaps even a late-season blizzard.

A good part of Morgantown already lay half-buried under the long winter's accumulation—houses that had been boarded up back in the fall and left empty for the season, others long ago abandoned when the old boom-camp days came to an end. Inhabited or empty, whether made of logs or of milled lumber hauled in across the passes, Morgantown's buildings clung to any patch of flatness, with haphazard flights of wooden steps running from one level to another and on down to the crooked street that twisted along the bottom of the gulch. A few straggling flakes of white were falling as Bannister reached this, and turned in the direction of the jail office.

He paused a moment to watch the snow spiral down against a drab background of unpainted buildings and rank, black mud and old drifts. When he moved on, the sound of his own boots on sodden plankings was loud in the curious stillness. Except for a horse that stood drooping its head over a hitch rail, he seemed the only living thing abroad in this last hour before the settling of dusk. Already a window or two showed lamplight.

In the slot of an alleyway between two dark buildings, just at his left, there was sudden muffled movement. A barrel thudded over, to a clatter of empty bottles and old cans—some prowling dog, he thought, and barely turned to look.

Instantly he halted, in mid-stride, seeing a pair of men who seemed to be bending over something on the ground; but it was the glimpse of a booted leg, lying toe up in dirty trampled snow, that tore an exclamation from him and sent him back that way at a run.

Frozen snowcrust squealed underfoot. Then he was booting aside spilled trash, and the men were straightening and whirling to stare at him through a fog of steaming

13

breath. He saw a lean face patched with red beard, and another with brows and eyelashes so pale that the scar slanting across the right cheek seemed to give it whatever expression it had. Both men wore the garb and the plain look of saddle tramps. Both were armed.

Bannister knew those faces—he had seen them around town often enough, throughout the long winter. Hauling up, he turned for a closer look at the figure sprawled at their feet. When he recognized the bulky buffalo coat, his eyes narrowed and his mouth set hard.

"So!" He raised his glance again to the pair standing over their victim. "I've been wondering what it would be, with you two," he said heavily. "I've just been watching to see. Somehow I didn't think it would be rolling drunks." He pointed to the fat pigskin wallet that the redhead held clutched in one rope-scarred hand. "Put it back where you got it, Clausen," he snapped. "Back in his pocket!"

Virg Clausen glared at him from under brows that were like a shelf above the bridge of a flat nose. Making no move to get rid of the wallet he ran his stare down Bannister's big frame, taking in the obvious fact that there was no gunbelt strapped on beneath the skirt of the Windbreaker.

This seemed to give him confidence. He straightened, chin tucked against chest, and a sneer began to shape his unshaven mouth. "Why don't you come and take it?" Deliberately he passed the wallet over to his left hand so as to leave his right hanging free, near the holster strapped to his own leg.

Bannister watched the movement of the other's hands. "You insist on having it this way?" he said coldly. "All right . . ." He started forward.

Instantly the blond man, Billy Ide, dropped into a crouch, one hand flicked inside his clothing and came out again holding a knife; the blade gleamed dully as it weaved slightly back and forth, its point trained at a spot just above Jim Bannister's belt buckle.

The latter halted again involuntarily, staring as sweat broke out on his body. He had no liking for knives; but Billy Ide, on the other hand, seemed partial to them. Perhaps that

14

accounted for the scar that pulled at his cheek, appearing to widen the grin of anticipation that drew the lips back and showed his teeth.

So, what now? Jim Bannister thought, while his belly crawled. He didn't consider himself a hero. Just pinning a badge on a man's shirtfront did not necessarily qualify him to pit sheer nerve and empty hands against an armed pair like this one.

A vagrant drift of snow came twisting down. The man in the buffalo coat lay, a sodden, motionless sprawl in the alley's filth; a faint reek of whiskey came from him.

Virg Clausen seemed amused at Bannister's hesitation. His sneer broadened. He indicated the man on the ground with a jerk of his chin. "You want to get killed for *that*, lawman? Tate Pauling—owner of the Tepee; the strong man of Morgan Valley! Six months ago, he had that damned black Irish foreman of his kick us off the ranch without an hour's notice. *Now* look at him!"

Bannister found his voice. "A lot can happen to a man in six months—or even less."

"Damn right!" Clausen looked with open scorn at the mud-daubed clothing, the slack face with its stubble of two-day beard. Tate Pauling's color was bad, and there was a trickle of drying blood down one grooved cheek. Even so, the blocky features, the stubborn jaw under the heavy mustache, still held a trace of arrogance and power.

The redhead grunted, "Is that what people around here used to jump for when he said 'jump'? Hell! He's what you just now called him: a plain, ordinary drunk!"

Bannister drew a breath. "It happens," he replied coldly, "that rolling drunks is a jailable offense in this town. And you're going to jail!" He took another deliberate step. He appeared to have dismissed Billy Ide and the knifeblade.

"By God, *no!*"

Virg Clausen screeched it. He backed away. His cheeks pinched; the muscle under one eye began to shake a little. His hand, its back matted with red fur, lifted to clamp the handle of the holstered gun.

Having made up his mind about what he was going to do,

Bannister had timed his moves to the last bare fraction of an instant. Now, even as Clausen drew, he pivoted directly away from him. A lunge brought him instead against Billy Ide, catching the blond man off guard.

Evidently Billy Ide had not expected the fight to come to him. His eyes widened in surprise, the grin lost its shape. And, with cold fear making him suck in his guts, Bannister used this brief moment's advantage to reach for the hand that held the knife.

He missed, felt the agonizing swipe of the blade's point across his palm. Desperately he waded ahead. His boot slipped on trampled mud; but now his big right fist traveled a short arc and struck the blond man a hasty, glancing blow. It landed, jerking his head around, causing it to bounce upon his neck.

In the next instant Bannister's fumbling left hand closed upon the sleeve of the man's coat. His fingers shifted again, located cold flesh and clamped down on it. Trying to ignore the blazing hurt of a slashed palm, he put all his muscle into the squeeze that brought a shriek from Billy Ide as the latter's hand crumpled. Bannister felt the fingers open, felt the knife handle strike his boot as it dropped.

Still holding Ide by that crushed hand he struck a second time and spurred by burning pain, a third. Billy Ide went limp and toppled backward over the upended trash barrel. Bannister let him go.

He had not forgotten his second enemy. Virg Clausen would have the gun by now, and he must not be allowed time to use it. Carried on by the momentum of his rush against Billy Ide, Bannister waded into the redhead. He saw the gun start to rise, saw the red-bearded face within inches of his own, caught the sour smell of whiskey. Teeth set against the pain of his injured hand, he seized the shoulder of a black and white mackinaw and threw Clausen around.

There was the shocking bellow of the sixgun at close quarters, but that had been only an involuntary pull of Clausen's finger at the trigger as the redhead was flung bodily against the peeled log wall beside them. His face struck the wood with a meaty sound; the hat tumbled from his head. And then Bannister had his gun arm, and he wrenched it up high between the man's shoulders. Clausen's knees sagged.

Bannister plucked the gun from unresisting fingers and let him go, and the redhead slid down the wall and to his hands and knees in a dazed crouch.

A stink of burnt gunpowder hung in the narrow alleyway. Breathing hard, Bannister stuffed the captured smoking weapon behind his belt, under the Windbreaker. He looked for Billy Ide, but the man was out cold; the knife lying in the snow where it had dropped. Sight of the deadly thing turned Bannister's knees a little weak. He bent and picked it up and savagely drove the point deep into a siding log. At his thrust the blade snapped off short and he flung the useless bone handle far from him.

Shaking a little, he decided again that a man had to be out of his mind to go unarmed against a knife and a gun.

Blood was dripping from the knife-slashed palm. Bannister fumbled out a handkerchief, bound the cut and used his teeth to fashion a clumsy tie. Afterward he hunted about for the pigskin wallet, found it on the ground; it was well padded with greenbacks. He shoved it for safekeeping into a pocket of his Windbreaker.

A glance at the wallet's owner showed him the man in the buffalo coat was stirring and making feeble efforts to sit up. Bannister got him under the arms and pulled him into position with his shoulders propped against the log wall, his head lolling drunkenly. That should do for the time being. Right now Tate Pauling would have to wait.

Bannister drew the gun as he turned to the redheaded prisoner. "On your feet," he ordered.

Virg Clausen lifted a face that was red and raw as a beefsteak, where it had slammed into the logs. "You go to hell!"

"I told you in the beginning you were headed for jail," Bannister reminded him. "You got a choice. You can go under your own steam—or I can always poleax you with this, and then drag you."

The redhead looked at the gun, and his mouth worked. He lifted his eyes to the big man standing over him. "I think you would, you bastard!" he gritted between his teeth. And,

17

clawing at the logs, he hauled himself to his feet. "But I'll settle this with you yet—don't think I won't. That's a promise, mister. Badge or no badge!"

"Your privilege to try,'" Jim Bannister snapped. "Get your friend," he ordered shortly. "He don't weigh much; you can carry him."

Protesting and threatening no longer, Clausen leaned and got a wrist-and-crotch hold on the unconscious Billy Ide, and straightened with the limp weight riding his shoulders. Bannister motioned the prisoner ahead of him, toward the street.

He had known that a single gunshot was certain to draw attention. Sure enough a small crowd was beginning to gather despite the cold, coming at a run from a half-dozen different directions. Men flung startled questions, which Bannister ignored; his mouth tight-clamped and eyes set straight ahead, he pushed his way through.

They gave way before him, but as he herded his prisoners toward the jail, a lengthening tail of the curious fell in at his heels. He could hear the thump of sodden planks underfoot and a growing babble of voices.

As Irene Youngdahl had said, there was little enough to break the monotony of life in a storm-locked town at the tag-end of dead winter. Realizing this, Bannister held onto his tongue and his temper.

A light was already burning in the marshal's office—a squat log building, with barred windows and a door enforced with strap-iron. He opened it and stood aside for Clausen to maneuver his way through, clearing the burden on his shoulders.

It was not much of an office. The windows were too small to give adequate light, and the stove was too small to heat it properly. A second door, opposite the entrance, opened onto the cell block at the rear.

For furnishings, Sam White had been able to collect a scarred flat-top desk and a few chairs, a filing case and a cabinet that held odds and ends of equipment, and an iron cot where his jailer slept. The wooden floor was icy cold; on a winter day, even with the stove working, a man sitting at

18

the desk would have to put his feet up on something or have them numb to the ankle.

The jailer, Bert Dakins, had his crossed on the edge of an open drawer, swivel chair tilted back while he shuffled through some old reward dodgers. A huge pile of these was stacked in front of him.

When he caught sight of the three who entered through the street door he dropped his feet and let the chair come forward with a clatter. He was a small man of about forty, with a suspicious ferret's face and a slight cast in one eye. Jim Bannister had been able to form no particular liking for the man, but he performed his routine duties well enough.

Now Bannister met his stare with a jerk of the head. "Get your keys," he said crisply. "I've brought us some customers."

Dakins stirred himself, tossed aside the dodgers he was holding, fumbled in the drawer and got out the cell-block keyring. In scrambling to his feet he jarred the stack of posters and they toppled. Pasteboard sheets bearing the pictures and descriptions of wanted men slid across the desk with a whisper, took the air and went skimming like a snowstorm in every direction. Bert Dakins let them go; Bannister and his prisoner trampled them underfoot, crossing the room to the other door which Dakins scurried to open.

Back here were a corridor and two small, dark cells. Dakins got a barred door open and Bannister marched Virg Clausen inside and helped him lay Billy Ide on one of the two bunks it held. Ide was beginning to recover from the blows that had laid him out. He groaned and opened his eyes for a moment, then closed them tight again. His jaw looked as though it would develop a swelling and a fine dark bruise where Bannister's fist had hit him.

Dakins, watching from out in the corridor, wanted to know: "What are they booked with?"

"I'll call it drunk and disorderly," Bannister answered crisply. "Also armed robbery and assault. That should hold them for a while." He came out of the cell, slammed the door to.

19

Dakins started to ask, "But who was it they—?"

"Tate Pauling. And I better get back out there to see that he's all right."

Virg Clausen had hold of the bars. "Damn you! What about Billy?" he demanded harshly. Bannister gave the blond man a critical stare.

"He looks like he's coming out of it. If he doesn't, I'll have Doc Barnhouse in to take a look." He swung about, then, to indicate the stove that stood in a cinder box at the end of the short cell-block hallway. "Build that fire up," he ordered Dakins, "and keep it going. I've spoken to you about that before. It's like an icehouse back here!"

The jailer, muttering, went to comply. Bannister had the keyring; he took it back into the office, and halted glowering at the men he found there.

He had almost forgotten about them. A good part of the crowd, having followed him in from outside, was still standing around in aimless curiosity and apparently hoping for some further scrap of excitement. Bannister was in no mood to indulge them. He went around behind the desk, dropped the keyring into its drawer and kneed it shut. He laid Clausen's captured sixgun on the wood. He looked at the handkerchief binding his cut; it would serve a little longer.

"All right," he grunted. "What happened out there doesn't concern any of you—all you're doing is letting a lot of cold air in. How about going on about your business? I mean it!"

Somebody swore half-heartedly, but he got no real argument as he herded them outside. About to follow, he saw something from the tail of his eye that halted him and turned him numb. Slowly he turned back, closing the door. He stood looking at the reward dodgers scattered over the room.

Head lifting, he called back to Bert Dakins, who could be heard rattling the shaker on the cell-block stove. "What's all this mess?"

"Huh?" The jailer appeared in the doorway, a piece of pine kindling in one hand and a smear of soot on his face.

20

He blinked at the litter on the floor. "Oh—them . . . I was cleaning out the storeroom. I found these old dodgers, and was just going through 'em before I threw 'em out. I'll pick 'em up—give me time. Hell, I can't do everything at once . . ."

Bannister neither saw nor heard him. Dakins, with an exasperated shrug, turned and went back to the stove that was giving him trouble. And Jim Bannister stooped, and from the scatter of pasteboards picked up the one that had been staring at him. There was a muddy heelprint where one of that crowd had walked on it, but it had not effaced the printing or the picture.

The face was his own. The bold block letters read: WANTED FOR MURDER. And below the picture:

JAMES BANNISTER

Height 6 feet 4 inches. Weight 220 pounds. Hair dark yellow, eyes blue. Convicted at Las Vegas, New Mexico for the murder of Wells McGraw, field representative of the Western Development Corporation of Chicago, Illinois. For the apprehension and capture of this man, DEAD OR ALIVE, Western Development Corporation will pay the sum of TWELVE THOUSAND DOLLARS.

Hard-eyed, Bannister looked toward that door where Bert Dakins had vanished. But, no—Dakins was not a good enough actor. Had he seen this there was no way on earth he could have kept from betraying the fact. Obviously, then, the man had been interrupted in time; Bannister's luck was still holding. But another thought stopped his breathing.

The thing had lain there, in the middle of the floor, in plain sight for any of that bunch of idlers to see during the minutes when he was busy putting his prisoners away. In which case—out in the dusk, or in one of Morgantown's saloons—someone could even now be spreading the news and talking up a posse. Unless he was hugging it to himself, nursing his courage, while he planned a way to make his play—from the back, perhaps—and collect that monstrous reward alone. . . .

Well, it was a nagging worry, but nothing new for a man grown used, by now, to living on the dodge. He drew a shallow breath, folded the piece of cardboard and shoved it into a pocket of his coat. A hasty search of floor and desk satisfied him there were no other copies, always barring the chance one might have left this room in somebody's pocket.

One precaution: Before he left the jail, he took a scarred leather belt and holster from the cabinet behind the desk and strapped them in place, below the skirts of the heavy coat. Drawing the gun and checking the loads he knew that from this moment, and as long as he remained in Morgan Valley, the weapon must stay with him. No longer could he enjoy the luxury of letting it hang on its peg inside that cabinet.

For four months he had laid it aside, except in line of duty. For four months he had been able, almost, to forget the insecurity and the aching loneliness of a man wronged by fortune and running from the law. It was a pleasant time, but it had been bound to end.

CHAPTER III

The crowd appeared to have scattered and gone to shelter, for once more the street had an empty look. Dusk was settling fast but the tentative fall of snowflakes still had not developed into anything more than that. A muted quiet lay over Morgantown.

In the alleyway where Bannister had had his empty-handed encounter against a knife and a gun, the man in the buffalo coat still huddled in a sprawl with his shoulders against the logs as he had been left. His head was tilted back and he was staring up stupidly at a quartet of men who stood as silently staring back.

Recognizing these men, Jim Bannister approached cautiously. He singled out one and told him crisply, "I don't want any trouble, Rickman. I think you'd all better get away from him!"

Four heads turned. Gil Rickman, a bitter-eyed man whose Bear Paw spread was a small and crowded neighbor of Tate Pauling's giant Tepee outfit, gave him a black look and said harshly, "We ain't hurting the son of a bitch any. Any hurt that's done, he's doing it to himself! When a man starts downhill—"

"He took a gunbarrel across the side of his head," Bannister corrected the rancher sharply. "He's lucky if he hasn't got a fractured skull." Down on one knee he made a more thorough examination than he had been able to before. He paid especial attention to a tear in the hurt man's scalp, just above the hair line, from which the blood had already ceased to run.

The stink of booze was strong enough. Tate Pauling must have spilled at least part of a drink on his muddy clothing.

Bannister straightened to his feet again. "Far as I can see, he's not too bad hurt; Doc Barnhouse is the one to say. But we better get him up from there before he takes pneumonia."

Gil Rickman said harshly, "Let him!"

"That's enough of that!" He looked narrowly at the four. Like their leader, Rickman, they were small ranchers—latecomers who had been pushed to the edges of Morgan Valley grass, hampered for years by Tepee's drift fences and Tate Pauling's arrogance. For them, understandably, the downfall of the man who dominated their existence in Morgan Valley was no unpleasant thing to see.

Bannister spoke to a gaunt and yellow-bearded man with the air of failure about him. "Stiegel," he said, "come over here and let's see if we can't put him on his feet."

Ira Stiegel hesitated, pale eyes shooting an uneasy glance at the others—he was weak, but Bannister knew he had a sense of fairness and for that reason had singled him out. Common decency won; the man shrugged off his friends' disapproval and shuffled forward to lend a hand. Together, he and Bannister got Tate Pauling under the

23

armpits, hoisted him out of the muck of the alleyway and onto his feet.

The Tepee owner was a good-sized, solid bulk of a man. With his legs under him he would have collapsed again if the others had not steadied him. But after that he pulled his head back, got it braced on his shoulders, and his dull eyes worked into focus. Bannister said, "The street's yonder, Tate. We'll help you."

"No!" Tate Pauling drew himself erect. With surprising strength, he swung his elbows and jerked free. "I want no help!" he said thickly, with a remaining trace of the proud arrogance that had long cast a shadow in Morgan Valley. "Damn it, let's go!"

Stiegel looked questioningly at Bannister, who shrugged. They stood back and watched Tate Pauling move unsteadily away without them. Afterward, slowly, the rest followed.

Tate Pauling made his uncertain way through that narrow slot between the buildings. Once he had to stop for a moment to steady himself against a log wall, until at last he came out to the street—and there he met disaster. In trying to lift a boot, he misjudged the distance and his toe failed to clear the edge of the planking; he fell solidly, despite a clumsy effort to catch himself.

Bannister heard Gil Rickman's bark of scornful laughter but ignored it. When Ira Stiegel would have gone forward he raised a hand, saying, "No—wait a minute. Maybe he'll make it on his own."

Sure enough, by the time they reached the sidewalk, Pauling had fought his way up to hands and knees, the bulky coat he wore making him look like an animal of some sort. But then, to a quick tapping of footsteps along the walk, he lifted his head and seemed to freeze.

The woman was tall for her sex, graceful of motion despite heavy winter clothing. One arm laden with packages, she halted, and Bannister could see her expression as her eyes met Tate Pauling's. Revulsion was there, and something more—hatred was almost not too strong a word for it.

Bannister said quietly, "Stella, he's been hurt. . . ." He saw this affected her. She had drawn her skirts back, as though unwilling to have them touch this man, but now her expression changed subtly. Compassion touched it—compassion for someone she had cause to hate as few others could.

Tate Pauling meanwhile was trying to get to his feet. He planted one boot under him, but then would have fallen again except that Jim Bannister had stepped forward in time and caught him.

Bannister lifted him firmly, steered him to a wooden bench set handily against the front of an adjacent store-building. Pauling dropped onto this and his head fell back against the wall so that it exposed clearly the blood that had dried in the stubble of his cheek.

Stella Harbord gave an exclamation: "Let me see that!" She put her bundles down and, drawing off a mitten, seated herself beside the man. She would have touched his face; but Pauling, suddenly wild-eyed, pulled away and turned his head away as far as he could. She stared at him, her hand poised.

"He won't let you," Bannister told her.

Behind them, someone guffawed heavily. Gil Rickman said, in harsh amusement: "You're looking at a guilty conscience!"

Bannister turned on him impatiently. "Isn't there anything better you could be doing?" he exclaimed. "Why don't the lot of you move on?"

"And why should we?" their leader retorted, coolly returning his look. "We're only watching. That's not breaking any law that I know of!" The tall man glared at him in exasperation but had no answer.

The interruption came from an unexpected quarter. No one appeared to have noticed the approaching sound of a buckboard's team or heard its wheels spinning over iron ruts until the rig was nearly upon them; and then it was a sudden angry bellow that pulled them around. Someone said, "Hell! There's that wild Irishman!" The buckboard rocked to a halt, the driver shouted again and a look of rage warped his face as he leaped down.

He was not too big a man, but he was solid. He had the black Irish coloring—the thick dark hair peppered with gray, though he could not have been much out of his thirties,

25

and the sharp blue eyes. His jaw was stubborn, his nose had a sideward crook to it as though it had been broken—probably in some bunkhouse duel—and never had properly knit.

The group let him shove in for a better look at Tate Pauling. He saw the blood on the man's face, and at once his fists were rising and his furious stare was searching from face to face.

"All right! What happened?" he demanded. "Which of you done this? Or did you all jump him. . . ."

"And supposing we did?" Gil Rickman answered with a leer, before anyone had a chance to deny it. A bellow broke from the Irishman's thick chest, and without any hesitation he waded in with fists cocked to swing.

Jim Bannister swore, and managed to get a shoulder in the way just in time to catch the charge and hurl the man back.

Grady Sullivan's boots lost purchase in a patch of ice and he had to fight for balance; this allowed Bannister a moment to turn on Rickman, saying, "Damn it, what's the matter with you? Do you *want* a fight? They had nothing to do with this," he told the Irishman. "None of them. Though it might serve this fellow right if I had let you go ahead and beat him up!"

"He could of tried," Rickman grunted, scornfully; nevertheless, he backed away a little.

What Bannister said appeared to have sunk in with the Irishman. Breathing hard, Sullivan ran a hand through his thick mop of hair, pushed it back. He was still angry and puzzled. "Somebody sure as hell better tell me what did happen! How'd Mister Pauling get bunged up like this?"

"He was jumped—back there in the alley—by a couple of drifters named Clausen and Ide."

The Tepee foreman scowled. "*That* pair! I knew they were no good. I had to fire them off the ranch, months ago."

"I know. They mentioned something about that—sounded like they hold a grudge. Anyway, they lifted this. Perhaps you'd better take care of it for your boss."

He brought out the pigskin wallet. Grady Sullivan's face darkened at sight of it. He grunted curt thanks as he took it

26

and dropped it in a pocket. "Where are they now?" he demanded harshly.

"In jail—thinking about the mistake they made. . . . Do you suppose we ought to see about getting Tate home—or to the doctor?"

"Yeah." The Irishman ran a big hand through his hair again. He suddenly looked tired. "I been out working cattle, checking the drift fences," he said heavily. "Got in today, and nobody at the ranch could tell me where Mister Pauling had gone to. I just hoped I'd find him here in town." He shook his head, drawing a breath. "You can't count on anybody any more. The crew has their orders—they know Mister Pauling is too sick to be let wander off alone this way."

"Sick!" Gil Rickman gave a snort. "That what you call it?" And one of the others—Dave Pitts—added: "I call it plain, falling-down drunk!"

Sullivan stiffened and fixed them each with his stare, in turn. "It's easy enough," he said finally, "to sneer at a man who's been put down for the count. But none of you has had a daughter you loved raped and murdered!"

At that thrust, Pitts broke gaze and slid his eyes away, uncomfortably. Not Rickman, however. Unabashed he retorted, "No, we never—and we never lynched the wrong man for it, either!"

Everything seemed to go very still, then; the stomping of the buckboard team, breaking the freezing crust of street mud, sounded suddenly loud. Grady Sullivan let out his breath in a plume of steam. Slowly, heads turned and they were all looking at the woman—all but Tate Pauling, who had let his chin sink upon his breast as though unaware of what went on around him.

"Miz Harbord," the Irishman blurted, "I ain't had the chance to say how damned sorry I am about your husband. I only wish to God I'd been here, and not off to Denver with a shipment. Was nothing I could do about Meg, of course—rest her soul; but I just might have been able to keep Mister Pauling from—from losing his head like he did. Maybe, the way he saw it, the evidence looked conclusive." The Tepee foreman spread his hands. "Still and all, it was a terrible

27

mistake and one that can't be undone. For whatever it's worth—I'm sorry."

Bannister, watching her averted face, could see that Stella Harbord had gone white and her hands knotted together in her lap. Then she lifted her head, put her level glance on the Irishman.

"You have no reason to apologize to me, Mister Sullivan. You had no part in what happened last fall. But I don't understand why I've never heard a word of explanation from Tate Pauling—not a single word, trying to excuse himself for what was done to my husband. . . ."

Sullivan could only shake his head and spread his hands. "I don't know, Miz Harbord. Except, maybe, some things are just too damned hard to say!"

"So he drinks himself into the gutter instead!" Gil Rickman grunted.

That touched the Tepee foreman off again. He whirled on the rancher, fists tightly clenched and voice shaking. "I got just one thing to say to you, you son of a bitch!" he told Rickman, through set lips. "And all the rest of you: It's no secret what's in your minds. You're like a damn pack of coyotes, setting on your haunches just waiting to catch the scent of carrion! Well, Tepee ain't dead—not by a long way. And you ain't gonna have the pleasure of tearing it to pieces. Not now, or ever!"

Gil Rickman had an odd, wedge-shaped face, wide at the temples and narrow in the jaw. His eyes held a shine of obsidian as they met the foreman's blazing stare. "Whatever gave you such a notion as that?" he demanded flatly.

Sullivan wagged his head at him. "All right—all right. You just remember what I'm saying. Mister Pauling still has him a crew, and he has me to rod it. So if you ask for war, you're gonna get one—just as bloody as you want!"

"Oh?" Rickman appealed to Jim Bannister, with a hunched shoulder and a faint smile that tilted a corner of his bitter, thin-lipped mouth. He spread his hands, shook his head a little. "*You* have any idea what this dumb Irishman is talking about?"

Goaded too far, the little man went after him then, with a wildly swinging fist that caught Rickman high on one cheekbone. It knocked him back, surprised, into the arms of his friends.

Someone cursed, and there was a startled outcry from the woman as Sullivan nearly scrambled over her, trying to follow and reach his enemy with another blow. Boots scuffled the plankings. Belatedly, Jim Bannister moved in to break up the fight.

He was enough bigger than the Irishman so that it was no real trouble to grab and haul him back, though Sullivan fought to get loose again. His hat fell from his head and he trampled it. Somewhere along the street a door slammed open. A man's voice shouted a question that went unanswered.

The brawl was already over before it began; the foreman subsided under Bannister's grip, with the latter's sharp command in his ears, and Bannister set him free.

Rickman had caught his balance by now. He had a gun strapped under the coat, but the lawman spoke a warning that stayed his hand. Glowering, Gil Rickman rubbed a palm across his mouth and looked at it as though to see if there was any blood. "By God!" he said hoarsely, over and over. "By God, for that I could—"

"You could what?" Jim Bannister prompted, eyeing him coldly.

The man subsided, and a careful mask moved across the fury in his face. But in that moment something had been revealed—a dangerous depth behind the colorless eyes and the bitter mouth that Bannister might never have suspected was there. He suddenly knew that Rickman was more than blustering talk and bad manners: he was someone to be watched.

The rancher must have seen the expression on Bannister's face, because his eyes narrowed a little. He moved his shoulders, demanding harshly, "You wouldn't be thinking maybe there's something to what he said just now?"

"About you neighbors of Tate Pauling's figuring to help yourselves to Tepee range?" Bannister let a blunt, appraising glance move across all their faces.

They met his look, except for Ira Stiegel who at the last
29

minute dropped his eyes away from it. Bannister cautioned:
"All I have to say is—he'd damn well better be wrong!"

Rickman stiffened. "And what business would it be of
yours, Bryan? You're only town law—temporary, at that.
You got no jurisdiction over anything that happens out in
the valley, so I hope you wouldn't try to take sides against
us—with a bastard like Tate Pauling!"

"I'm on one man's side only," Bannister answered
curtly. "Sam White's. As deputy sheriff, the valley *is* his
jurisdiction. Long as I'm standing in for him here in
Morgantown, I'll stretch the town limits if I have to,
protecting his interests and his job. I can't afford to care
whose toes I might step on when I do it."

For a hostile moment Gil Rickman's stare measured the
length of this tall stranger. He said then, from a mouth like a
trap, "That's easy talk—but you ain't rightly showed
anybody what you got to back it up with. Someone should
warn you, mister: If it comes to stepping on toes, no man's
too big to be squashed . . . not even Tate Pauling, and
certainly not *you*!"

Abruptly, then, he shouldered the little Irishman aside
and was gone at a hard stride along the dusky street. The
men who had let him do their talking for them hesitated
briefly, then with an uneasy exchange of looks went after
their leader. Bannister let them go; nothing would be served
by prolonging this.

He looked at Stella Harbord, seated on the bench beside
Pauling, her face drained colorless, eyes watching Bannister. He shook his head at her and let out the trapped
breath from his lungs as he turned to Grady Sullivan, who
was just straightening from picking up his fallen hat. In a
quiet voice the foreman said, as he pulled it on, "I'll be
driving Mister Pauling home, now. Maybe you'll help me
get him into the buckboard."

"Maybe we ought to have Doc Barnhouse see him. It
doesn't look to me he's bad hurt, but—"

"Anything Mister Pauling needs, I can give him," the little foreman said stubbornly, and Bannister let it go.

Together they managed to lift Pauling to his feet, get his
steps directed toward the buckboard. The rancher walked

30

between them like a somnambulist, seemingly indifferent where they guided him. Sullivan climbed up onto the seat and with some effort his boss was hoisted up beside him. He sat there, a solid lump.

Wind buffeted the steep gulch street, whipping a swirl of snowflakes into their faces, making the waiting horses stomp. "I'll get my horse and ride along with you," Bannister offered.

"I can manage." The reins in his hands, Grady Sullivan peered down at the tall man, past the sodden figure of his boss. His voice turned suddenly fierce. "I been managing for Mister Pauling a hell of a long time. I punched herds for him, over the Chisholm and the Goodnight, when I wasn't much more than a kid on my first riding job. And I been with him ever since. I been with him here in Morgan Valley for ten years—ramrodding, for eight. We built a fine spread, Mister Pauling and me. Don't ever forget it!"

There was a loyalty in the little man that Jim Bannister could not help but like. He said, "Nobody's forgetting that, Sullivan—just because the man's fallen into some bad personal problems."

"Is that what you think? Well, I can tell you—you couldn't be farther wrong! That wasn't all talk, just now. There's hell brewing in this valley."

He was probably right, Jim Bannister thought. Everyone seemed to know it. Even mild-mannered Lloyd Canby had said something like it at the council meeting an hour ago.

Bannister kept his voice quiet as he said, "Maybe you better understand this: I don't like Tate Pauling, and I hold no brief for him *or* his enemies. I've got just one interest in all this, and you already know what it is. Just remember it—because I'd hate to have to come after you!"

The foreman looked at him for a long moment. Then he nodded. "All right—all right, Mister Bryan. We've both made ourselves clear. If it's war, I'm gonna have to look out for Tepee—whatever you might do, and whatever it might do to Sam White. Sorry, but that's how it is."

He turned away, then, and ended the talk by slapping leather on the backs of the team. Jim Bannister stepped back as Sullivan yelled his horses into a tight turn that

31

cramped the wheels and made the rig lurch and tilt over the frozen ruts, while Tate Pauling swayed groggily but kept his seat. Then Sullivan had his rig straightened out and he sent it rolling away into the gathering night, back toward the valley and Tepee headquarters.

Jim Bannister raised a hand and drew it across his jaw, frowning and thoughtful. He turned, then, as Stella Harbord came up beside him, carrying her parcels. She started to say, "Jim, do you think—?" but then she saw the makeshift bandage. "Why, you're hurt!"

"Just a cut." But she seized his hand, turned it palm upward.

"That looks bad to me, Jim. You come with me—I'm going to fix it for you!"

He hesitated, then nodded tiredly. A troubled hardness was in his voice as he answered, "All right, Stella. I need some words with Sam White, anyway. . . ."

CHAPTER IV

Sam White's shack—steep-roofed, unpainted—perched on a rocky level some distance above the street. Bannister followed the woman up a zigzag of wooden steps to the door, carrying her packages for her, and into the warmth of the drab living room where a fire had been left banked in the space heater that sat in one corner.

The furnishings were sparse and looked like discards—a round, marble-topped table with a lamp on it, a sagging rocker, an old horsehair sofa that Stella had made do for a bed during these months as Sam's nurse and housekeeper. Doors led off to Sam's bedroom and to the kitchen. Aside from a lean-to at the back, for a pantry, that was all there was.

Bannister stood waiting, while Stella Harbord threw off her wraps and got the lamp lighted. As its yellow glow spread and the glass shade clinked into place, there was the

32

sound of bedsprings under a turning body, and through the bedroom's half-open door came an old man's voice: "Stella . . . ? Who's with you?"

"It's Jim," she answered, "he's been hurt. I brought him here to fix it up." Bannister had put the packages on the table and now he followed her as she carried the lamp into the bedroom. Its light, flowing ahead of them, showed them the figure in the bed and the gaunt face under its tangle of thinning hair.

Sam White had seen the bloody handkerchief. His sharp black eyes lifted to Bannister's face, holding a question, as Stella put the lamp on the dresser, fixed the pillows and helped the old man to a sitting position.

Bannister said, "It's nothing much, really—a little trouble over a knife. I had to disarm a drunk." He didn't elaborate and the lawman in the bed appeared satisfied, not asking any further details or even the name of the troublemaker—far from trying to run things from his sickbed. When he turned over the affairs of his office, Sam White had done a thorough job of it.

Jim Bannister took this as partly a sign of the older man's trust and confidence; but there was something more to it— strange lassitude and failure of interest that sometimes worried him.

Stella Harbord said, "Come in the kitchen, Jim, I'll see what needs to be done."

"One moment, first." From his pocket he took the reward dodger he had brought from the jail. He unfolded it. "Sam, do you remember seeing this before?"

Sam White put out a hand for it. He frowned; his ragged gray mustache pushed forward above pursed lips. "Yes," he said finally. "Yes, I do, come to think of it. I'd forgotten receiving a dodger on you. It must have been at least a year ago. Where did you run across it—at the jail?"

Bannister nodded, while the woman watched them both with an anxious expression. Wind, blowing down the gulch, pummeled the walls of the shack and a draft stirred the curtains at the window. Bannister said, "Bert Dakins turned up a bunch of these things somewhere and this was one of them. I have an idea he never actually saw it himself. But there were other men in and out of the room, and it was lying in plain sight."

He saw the alarm, as this sank in. He refolded the stiff paper, returned it to his pocket. "I was just wondering if there could be any more copies around?"

"It's possible," the old man admitted, moving his head on the pillow. "Every once in a while I get duplicates. . . . What if another does show up?" he demanded. "Or supposing somebody did happen to see this one? What will you do?"

"Hard to say. What may be more to the point—what will *you* do? It could look very bad for you."

Sam shrugged. "We've both known the risks. Besides, how could I be expected to remember every face on every wanted notice that comes into my office?"

"Not many are good for twelve thousand dollars!" Bannister pointed out. "And the fact remains, you *did* know who I was the minute you laid eyes on me in the hills last fall. You'd seen my picture in the Denver papers, and yet you said nothing. Instead, when that accidental bullet in your leg put you out of action, I ended up as your substitute in the marshal's job. An enemy could make something of that!"

Stella exclaimed, "But Sam has no enemies!"

He looked at her, somber with the recollection of that council meeting. "Every man has enemies. It's that kind of a world!"

The old man spoke. "When I gave you this job, Jim, I told you where I stood. I said I didn't care a damn for syndicate law. I said I believed your version of what the syndicate's guns did to you down there in New Mexico— taking your spread, killing your wife. I still think it was a guilty conscience made that McGraw fellow pull his gun when you cornered him, and forced you to kill him."

"A jury decided otherwise. They said I murdered him. There's a hangrope still waiting for me down at Vegas."

"And it can wait! I don't think you're a murderer and I see no reason all at once to start acting as though I did—not just because this damn thing has suddenly turned up." He nodded toward Bannister's pocket.

34

Bannister's chest swelled with gratitude. He said gravely, "I won't bother to thank you again, Sam. You owed me absolutely nothing; and you know what you were offering: A chance to forget about running—for a while; a place to hole up in safety, even for these few months the passes would be closed."

"No thanks needed," the other said gruffly. "You figure I haven't come out ahead on the deal? Maybe it ain't been a relief and a comfort, knowing the job at the jail is in hands I can trust while I'm laid up!"

"But, surely, it must be time you were on your feet?" Bannister demanded, quickly. "Shouldn't you be about ready to take over again?"

Sam's answer was evasive. "Sure—sure. One of these days." He lifted a hand, let it fall back onto the counterpane. "Afraid I'm beginning to realize I'm not as young as I was, Jim. Just don't seem to have the spit I used to; it's taken the sickness, and the winter, to make me feel it. And since you've got things under control. . ."

Jim Bannister knew this was the moment—right now— to tell him about the scene in Youngdahl's parlor. Shock of knowing what was going on behind his back might be the best thing in the world to rouse Sam White and stir him out of this odd lethargy. And yet, it seemed a pitiless treatment for a tired and sick old man. Somehow Bannister couldn't bring himself to it.

He tried a different tack:

"You have to realize I may not be around much longer. I'll have to leave, once the passes open. Maybe, because of this," he tapped his pocket, "even sooner. It's only wise— for both of us."

The sick man waggled his head like a badgered bull. "I understand," he said in a tired voice. "But, please, don't push me, Jim! Stella keeps trying to push me. I tell you, I'm just not up to it yet. . . ."

His eyes closed, his head sank back upon the pillow. Jim Bannister looked across him, in some exasperation, at the woman and saw her frown and troubled shake of head. She turned away and, getting no further response from Sam, he followed her out of the room.

35

In the kitchen, Stella had a lamp going and was bustling about, feeding wood into the big range, moving the teakettle forward from the back of the stove to heat. Bannister said, "I don't like to see him this way. I don't quite know what to make of it."

She paused in her work. "Well—he's not a young man, Jim. And he's been very ill. . . ."

"But isn't it time he was getting better? I know Doc Barnhouse thinks so."

"So do I. But sometimes, after you've had a siege like that, I think it takes some extra incentive—some special push—to put you on your feet again. I'm beginning to wonder what it will take his case. Right now I want to fix that hand."

He considered the problem of Sam White, while Stella gathered the materials she needed—a clean dishtowel that she tore into strips, a tin basin to hold water from the steaming teakettle, a bottle of antiseptic.

Jim Bannister removed his Windbreaker and rolled back his sleeve. She motioned him to a chair at the cheap, oilcloth-covered deal table and, seated opposite him, unwound the handkerchief from his wounded hand.

Dried blood had stuck the cloth to his palm and it had to be soaked loose. She worked gingerly, lower lip caught between her teeth. "It doesn't really look too serious," she finally said, when she had the bloody cloth removed. "But I'll have to clean it out and put something on it. That will hurt."

"Go ahead," Bannister said. "I didn't expect it would be a picnic. . . ."

Even so, she was wonderfully gentle; and Bannister became so engrossed in watching the quick efficiency of her strong, firm hands that the pain she caused him became a secondary thing. She worked in silence, her brow puckering as she pulled the cut wide and dabbed at it carefully while the water in the basin turned pink. Afterward, the antiseptic made him wince and set his jaw, but he shook his head at her quick questioning look. "It's all right," he said. "You're a good nurse."

"You are a very good patient," she answered. "Better

than some I could name." He knew she meant the old man in the other room; he could guess the trial old Sam must have been for her during this winter he had been in her care.

He looked at the top of her brown head, bent anxiously forward, at the clean white line of the part and the thick mass of her hair where the lamplight found coppery tints. And he was struck, for the hundredth time, by this reminder of his dead wife Marjorie—killed when the syndicate gunmen used force to put them off their little horse spread in New Mexico.

But that was nearly two years ago, and many hundred miles away. It was the past, and could never be recovered; and though lately it had bothered him to realize that he could no longer clearly picture that dead girl's face, suddenly he felt that there was no disloyalty in the fact.

Nor would Marjorie have considered it so; all at once he was sure of it. She was dead, but he was alive—and so was the woman who sat across the table from him. They were both part of a vibrant, living present. . . .

Conscious, suddenly, that Stella's brown eyes had lifted to his own, he saw her expression and stirred himself out of these thoughts. He said, "Is something the matter?"

"No." She shook her head a little. "It's just that—I find you sometimes looking at me strangely."

He was embarrassed. He shrugged and said, a little gruffly, "It's not so strange. After all, I'm a lonely man." At that a tinge of color mounted to her cheeks. She started to say something, her lips parting. Then in confusion she dropped her eyes and would not look at him again until the job was finished.

As she bound the palm in a clean strip of cloth she said, "This should at least keep it free of infection. If you have any trouble perhaps you'd better see Henry Barnhouse. He might decide you need a stitch or two."

"All right. But it feels fine. Thanks again for your trouble."

She rose without answering and cleared the table of the things she had been working with. At the sink, her back to Bannister, she asked, "Will you eat with us? I'll be fixing something shortly."

"I'd like to," he said, "but I'd better not. I left Bert Dakins in charge at the jail, and I should be checking in." He got his coat from the back of the chair, his hat off the floor beside it. But then he stood a moment, holding them, looking at the woman.

"Stella," he said suddenly, "the Lord knows I have no right to make it my business; I'm the last man in the world who should try to give anyone else advice. No difference. We've become good friends, in these months, and I can't help feeling concerned."

Turning, she looked at him now. "About me?"

"Just what will you do, once your job as Sam White's nurse is finished? I know you have no money. And I can't believe there's anything for you in Morgantown, not after —"

"After they killed my husband?" she finished. "That's true enough," she admitted, slowly. "I only came to this town because Luke thought there might be a chance for him here at something better than a bar-room card table. Instead all he found was a rope that belonged around another man's neck. . . ."

She turned her face away, suddenly, her expression bitter despite the months she had had to get over the shock of her husband's death at the hands of a posse that Sam White, with a bullet in his leg, had been unable to control.

Jim Bannister could understand her feelings. Luke Harbord might not have been much—a coward and a fiddle-footed gambler who had forfeited the right to whatever love his wife had once felt for him. But what had been done to him was too terrible to wish on any man. That Meg Pauling's actual murderer had been found and punished—too late—did nothing to change that.

Stella had recovered her composure. Straightening her shoulders, she pushed the hair away from her forehead and continued: "No, I hadn't thought much about where I'll go from here. Denver, or Kansas City perhaps—it doesn't matter much. I'll get by; I always have." She looked directly at Bannister. "But—when *you* go, it starts all over again for you—the running, and the hiding, and the danger. Somehow I just can't bear the thought!"

38

He lifted his shoulders. "A man can get used to almost anything."

"But, not *that*—not ever! Surely not!" Her eyes were wide and grave. "I would say there has to be hope, somewhere at the end of the line."

"I've got hope. After all, I know I killed Webb McGraw in self-defense; and knowing that, there's got to be some way to square myself with the law, and with the syndicate. . . ."

"But, without any witnesses—?"

Doggedly he continued. "I've got to have the hope, Stella. What else do you think keeps me in this country, here in the middle of my enemies? Why do you think I haven't tried running for Mexico or South America—any place where I might bury myself away, even from the syndicate? Trouble is, that's not what I want either." His lips quirked, in a half smile of quiet irony. "Come to think of it, in a way I'm sort of like Luke Harbord: I just want a clean slate and a new deck of cards.

"God only knows, in the long run, if I'll have any better luck than he did, getting it. . . ."

CHAPTER V

The founders of Morgantown, in desperate need of building material and lumber for their mine workings, had all but stripped this gulch of its timber. But there was some second-growth stuff, on a snowy spur a quarter mile or more from the jail, and it was here that Jim Bannister had come this morning seeking wood for the stoves at the jail. He had found a lightning-killed pine of a size he could handle and was working on it with an axe, favoring as much as he could that bandaged left palm.

Last night's weather had cleared away, and the sky was scoured a clean shining blue of incredible depth. It was just cold enough to make a man enjoy the expenditure of energy as he swung the axe, hearing the thin echoes of the strokes leap back at him off the mountain faces. Through the film of his own breath he could see the sweep of snowfields, and Morgantown crammed into the gulch beneath a shelf of chimney smoke. There was almost no wind.

Presently Bannister paused in his labor, as his bay horse, tied in the trees, nickered and pawed loose snow. Straightening, he saw a rider approaching over the trail he had broken up the face of the spur. The horse was a trim black mare; the shape of the rider, too small for a man, quickly resolved itself into that of Irene Youngdahl. She was riding sidesaddle in a well-fitted riding skirt, warm coat, and with a fur cap placed carefully atop her sleek blond head. Bannister sank the axebit into the trunk of the tree he was working on, and turned as she drew to a halt.

The black was restive and danced about a little, raising a spume of powder snow. The woman spoke to it roughly, and settled it with the reins; this brief flash of anger, smoothing out abruptly as she turned to Bannister, had revealed a side of her nature she probably did not realize had betrayed itself.

Her manner was bland enough as she said, "You seem to be the busiest man! I don't think I've ever seen you when you weren't working at something or other. Don't you ever take any time off? Even on Sunday?"

Bannister shrugged. "It's not that kind of a job. . . . You bound for somewhere?"

"Just a ride. Up the valley trails an hour or two, for the exercise." She indicated the bay, with a nod of her golden head. "Do you suppose you could be persuaded to keep a lady company?"

"Why me?" He was surprised at the suggestion, and then a shade irritated.

"I told you yesterday that I find you intriguing, Mister Bryan. I'd like a chance to—get acquainted."

Something in her voice gave the invitation a subtle suggestiveness. It was not lost on Bannister; neither was the direct challenge of her eyes. There was a physical pull about this woman that could be an exciting thing, given the proper circumstances. He felt this, but did not respond. Instead it

40

angered him, yet something warned him not to make his refusal too blunt.

He indicated the axe. "I'm already getting my exercise. And when I'm finished here, I'm afraid I've got other things waiting. We're not all of us free to drop everything and change our plans on the spur of the moment. It's too bad."

The woman looked at him with a level stare that hid whatever was behind it and made him uncomfortable. "Yes—isn't it!" she said finally, and touched a spurred heel to the flank of her black mare. She rode on, without another word or glance, cutting off down the thinly snow-covered slope to fall into the trail that swept away up-valley.

Bannister stood and watched until the first pines swallowed her, thinking: What would Claude Youngdahl have to say if he'd overheard this? He wondered how much her husband really knew—or cared—about her habits. Scowling slightly, he reached for the axe, jerked its bit loose from the wood, and fell to again.

Presently his blade found the hollow core of the blasted pine and it toppled, sending up a small cloud of loose snow. He trimmed some of the branches, then lashed the axe to his saddle. Afterward he took down his rope, tied on, and mounted to snake the log downslope behind his bay horse. A quarter hour later, having unsaddled and put his horse in the shed at the rear, he walked into the jail.

Bert Dakins, in his flannel undershirt, was shaving before a mirror that was propped on a couple of nails driven into the wall. The jailer gave him a sour look and a nod as Bannister told him, "There's some wood in the side lot. I went and got it; I'll leave it for you to work up into stove lengths."

"All right."

"Don't forget; it's apt to get pretty cold in here. There's not enough in the box to last us another night."

"Said I'd get around to do it, didn't I?" the other grumbled. Bannister let it go at that, and went back to see his prisoners.

They were eating breakfast from the tin plates Dakins had passed under the door to them. Except for the fresh scabs on Virg Clausen's face, where it had scraped rough log siding, neither looked much the worse for last night's fight. Seated on the cell's two bunks, shoulders bent over the plates on their knees, they stopped wolfing their food long enough to glare at Bannister.

He said, "Looks like the pair of you had done some sobering up since last night."

Billy Ide's lips quirked; the shining knife scar on his cheek pulled his mouth into an ugly shape. "Go to hell!"

"How long do you think you can hold us here, mister?" the redhead demanded. "Till spring thaw?"

"That's something that has to be worked out," Bannister answered calmly enough. "When I know the answer, I'll tell you."

"I told you last night," Clausen said heavily, "these bars, and that piece of metal on your shirt, don't change anything between us. We got a settlement coming. Don't you forget it!"

"You remind me," Bannister said. He left them to their sullen meal, and went out through the jail office with a final word of instruction for Bert Dakins. Leaving the building, he followed the twisted street to the big, two-storied hotel where he had his room and kept his few personal belongings.

In winter the hotel maintained a limited operation, with its upper story closed off, catering to only a half dozen permanent guests—like Bannister—on a seasonal basis. His room, like the hotel, had been a fairly presentable one back in the boom-camp days but was rundown now; the stained wallpaper was badly faded, and the carpet had had trails worn into it by the passage of many boots. But the bed was comfortable, and it was the nearest thing to a home Bannister had known in many months. He found nothing to complain of.

In the closet hung his one good suit of clothes, an extravagance paid for out of his scanty salary. He took it out and laid it on the bed, then cleaned himself up and polished his boots with a rag, whistling tunelessly as he worked. Afterward, dressed in his best, he smoothed down his stubborn yellow hair with the palms of big, rope-tough, horse-wrangler's hands—one with a bandage to remind him

42

of that grim business in the alley last evening—and surveyed himself critically in the spotted mirror.

That craggy face, with its long lips and solid jawline, should rightly bear the signs of some of the things this man had been through; but they just were not there. He did not look like someone on the dodge, who had seen his way of life destroyed and himself harried by all the power of a million dollar combine, and who traveled still with the shadow of a rope upon him. Perhaps there was a wary caution in the look of the quick blue eyes; but aside from that, it was amazing that so much could happen and mark a man so little—outwardly.

And here he was, embroiled in the muddled affairs of Morgan Valley, and the end of it not in sight. He shrugged a little, and reached his hat off the brass bedpost. It was the only hat he owned, and its sweat-stained shapelessness contrasted with the new shine of the suit. He batted it against his knee, to knock some shape into it, and smiled wryly at the effect as he drew it on.

The bell at the meeting house was sending its strokes through the stillness, reminding Morgantown what day it was. When Bannister climbed the steps to Sam White's door Stella was waiting, her Bible in one gloved hand; smiling, she tucked the other into the crook of his arm. She was graceful of movement, tall for a woman. It touched him with pride to have her walk beside him and join the movement of townspeople toward the Sunday morning services.

Despite the chill, people stood about in the snow in front of the church, chatting and reluctant to leave the bright sunshine. Here and there men nodded to Bannister, touched their hatbrims to the woman beside him.

The lean, sandy-haired preacher, who doubled on weekdays as schoolmaster for the valley's children, stood bareheaded in the doorway and shook Bannister's hand. Entering, he escorted Stella to one of the rough wooden pews.

The church was plain enough, lacking stained glass, though it did boast a small pump organ that had been freighted across the passes. But Jim Bannister, though

43

himself not a particularly religious man, liked to come here—even to take his uncertain part in the singing of the hymns.

This Sunday ritual had come to mean a great deal to him, for here he felt accepted and part of this community. In such a friendly atmosphere he could almost forget that it was only temporary—a world and a kind of life he must all too soon leave behind him.

But now Sid Noon, the livery man, came down the center aisle with his wife; his eyes met Bannister's and at once turned hard, and the man's mouth drew down, the lips pinched tight with an expression of pure hostility.

Reminded of the cross currents that had been set in motion at that council meeting yesterday Bannister returned the look with a nod, but the day had lost some of its warmth. Pure imagination, he told himself. Yet, suddenly, every place he looked he felt he could detect signs of unfriendliness. When he nodded to Lloyd Canby, the storekeeper ducked his head as though in embarrassment.

No question about it—there really was a difference; overnight, somehow, the atmosphere had changed.

The minister's wife began to play the introduction to a hymn. As Bannister leaned to take a hymnal from the rack in front of him, he experienced such an overwhelming sense of the pressure of eyes resting on him that, almost without willing to, he turned his head. Black eyes in a dark and bearded face locked with his own.

The man's name was Hodem—he was the town's blacksmith, stocky of build and with the massive shoulders and powerful hands of his trade. His stare rested unwavering on Bannister's and held until the latter turned away from it, more shaken than he cared to admit.

There had never been any trouble between himself and Reub Hodem; no reason to read a threat into a casual meeting of looks. . . . But all at once he remembered that last evening the blacksmith had been part of that crowd who had watched the arrest of Ide and Clausen and had followed along to the jail where reward dodgers lay scattered over the floor.

And, remembering, Bannister could not deny the icy lump that knotted hard and tight inside him.

Tate Pauling had built his Tepee headquarters on a long bench, with the timbered hills rising behind it, and a good sweep of the valley stretching below. It was an imposing view.

This range was watered by the lifeline of a single good-sized creek that later left the valley in an unnavigable, whitewater rush through a slot it had cut in the southern end. Here it lay wide and placid, frozen over now except for a narrow center channel that sent back the reflection of the sky and the winter sun.

Bannister drew rein to peer at the brightness and dazzle of snow-covered bottom land. It stretched to the far valley wall, etched in black by scattered stands of timber, or by the leafless line of alders and willows along the river and the hollows, and broken by an occasional straight-ruled line that was a fence.

In the middle distance, a pair of cowpunchers on a horsedrawn sledge were forking cut hay to a bunch of Tepee cattle clustered about them in the broken snow. Now and then a burst of laughter, or a low bawling from the animals, came thinly across the stillness.

At this late season the Morgan Valley ranchers would be scraping pretty close to find feed for their herds. There looked to be several good stacks left in the Tepee stack-yards that Bannister could see from this vantage point some half dozen miles away, but no cattleman ever felt certain he really had enough. An unusually prolonged season, or a late freak blizzard—even, perhaps, an accidental destruction of his feed stacks—could mean disaster. Nothing, except the coming of spring, and the final melting of the snows could assure him that he had indeed managed to weather one more of these treacherous Rocky Mountain winters.

Jim Bannister rode on to the ranch headquarters, a complex of buildings and corrals, with the big log-and-fieldstone ranchhouse dominating the rest of the layout. A line of barren cottonwoods rimmed the yard, standing gaunt against the black-and-white slope beyond.

Smoke rose bluely from a half dozen chimneys; at the horse corral, cowhands were roping out fresh mounts for themselves. Even on a Sunday, in dead of winter, this was a bustling and a busy place.

As Bannister dismounted at the house and wrapped his reins about the tiepole, a couple of horsemen were angling across the work area in the direction of the stock barn. One of them was the foreman, the black-haired Grady Sullivan.

At sight of Bannister he pulled rein sharply, spoke to his companion, passed him the reins of his own horse and stepped down. As the puncher rode away leading the animal, Sullivan came walking over, his bootheels squealing on packed snow. His broad face was suspicious.

"I never seen you out here before, Marshal," he said bluntly. "Ain't this outside your bailiwick?"

"A piece," Bannister answered calmly. "All the same, I have business. I'd like to see your boss."

Sullivan studied him a moment, then shrugged and motioned him toward the steps. He let Bannister precede him across the veranda, let him open the door; following inside, the Irishman shoved the heavy door closed with his shoulder.

Someone who didn't know Tate Pauling might have learned a great deal about him, from standing here in the living room of his home. The man's arrogance and pride showed in the massive ugliness of the furnishings, and in the very size of the room which was long enough to have a huge stone fireplace at each end.

A rack held a couple of Winchester rifles and a shotgun; a saddle lay against one wall with a huge elkhead mounted above it. The floor, bare except for a couple of throw rugs, had once been good; but it, and the stairs leading to a second story, were ruined from the scoring of countless dragging spurs.

There was no feminine trace whatever to suggest that Tate Pauling's wife had ever lived and died in this house, or that a daughter had grown up here. Bannister, looking about him, thought of the brief life and tragic death of poor, murdered Meg Pauling, and what an oppressive place it must have been for a sensitive and unhappy youngster to have to call her home.

It seemed cold and unfriendly, despite the blaze roaring in one of the big fireplaces.

He turned to Grady Sullivan, who was regarding him with that look of sullen suspicion. "Well, what is it?" the foreman challenged him. "One of that bunch I tangled with last night want me arrested, maybe?"

Bannister shook his head, a little impatient. "You really ought to take the chip off your shoulder," he said. "It's nothing like that—and I wouldn't have obliged them if it was. No, this has to do with the pair that jumped your boss. Clausen and Ide."

"Yeah?" The Irishman seemed only slightly mollified. "What about them?"

"I'm afraid it's something I have to take up with Tate."

"You can't do that. Mister Pauling ain't feeling so good today."

After last evening, Bannister could well believe it. But he insisted: "Sorry to hear it. All the same, I have to find out what he intends doing about the two I've got sitting in the jail. Does he want them held for trial?"

"Damn right he does!" Sullivan answered promptly. "Those bastards could of killed him! They're to get what they got coming."

"All right, then he's going to have to swear a formal complaint. Otherwise I have no choice but to turn them loose."

Sullivan's sharp blue eyes narrowed. "You mean—you'd just open the jail door and let that pair walk out?"

"That's the law. Twenty-four hours is the longest I'm allowed to hold any man on an open charge. So if Pauling wants them held, I'll need his statement of charges. That's why I came this afternoon—thought I could save him a trip to town."

"Now, hold on a minute!" The Irishman raised a broad, rope-scarred hand. "Let's get a few things straight; I ain't so much on these legal ins and outs. . . . Supposing Mister Pauling takes them into court, will he have to testify?"

Bannister nodded. "Law says a man's entitled to be confronted by his accuser. In person."

"I see. . . ." At this a weight of deliberation seemed to settle on the other, corrugating his brow into a scowl. He swung away from Bannister, took several strides across the spur-scored acres of uncarpeted floor and came to a stand beside a big table with lion-claw feet whose dusty surface was littered with newspapers and old stock catalogues and a length of hemp rope. He ran a hand across his face, fingered the battered nose. Then he struck the table with his knuckles and turned again to the other man.

"Reckon you better go ahead and set 'em loose, then!"

Bannister stared. "You want me to let them go?"

"You heard me!"

He shook his head. "That's a change of tune!" he said. "But, the fact remains it's not for you to say. It's still Tate Pauling's decision."

At that, Grady Sullivan strode toward him angrily. He was far below the other's height but at that moment he seemed unaware of it. Fists clenched, he said, "I'm making it my decision, Bryan! Mister Pauling's not a well man. It would go against my conscience if I was to let him walk into a courtroom."

"It might be weeks before the passes open," Bannister pointed out. "Longer than that, before the case has a chance to get on the docket. By that time—"

The blue eyes blazed. "Do I have to spell it out for you? Damn it, I won't have him humiliated! If Mister Pauling goes on the witness stand and a judge starts asking him questions under oath, it will *all* have to come out. How, last night, he was—was—"

"How I was blind, staggering drunk?" a new voice cut in.

They both turned, startled. Tate Pauling stood on the stairs, leaning heavily on the railing. He was in a nightshirt and a heavy woolen bathrobe, his feet encased in carpet slippers—which explained how he could have made his way down the steps, unheard. He looked bad. His grizzled hair was uncombed; stubborn jaw was unshaven; eyes were hollow caverns in a gray, hungover mask of a face. The arm that supported his weight upon the stair rail shook visibly.

Grady Sullivan recovered the use of his tongue. "Mister

48

Pauling!" he exclaimed hoarsely. "Why are you out of bed? You ain't in any shape to be up like this, and—"

Tate Pauling gave his foreman no more than a contemptuous glance. "Grady Sullivan's an idiot!" he told Bannister flatly, and the foreman's face turned slowly red. "If I want to take on a load and make a fool of myself it's my affair, and I don't need anybody covering for me. Let the world know it—why should I give a damn? I ain't even queasy about owning to it in court, if there's anything to be gained.

"But in this case, it just ain't worth the trouble. A couple of cheap saddle tramps—hell, I can't be bothered! Certainly not, if it means going clear to the county seat for a trial."

"Bryan did get the money back," Grady Sullivan ventured to agree, though he still showed the sting of his boss's manner. "And that's really the important thing."

Pauling merely shrugged as if to say a few dollars in a wallet were not important at all. Jim Bannister tried to keep the cold dislike for the man out of his voice. "Are you saying you don't intend to prosecute?"

The rancher made an arrogant gesture with his free hand—but the hand trembled noticeably. "Turn them out. Understand, though, I expect you to see to it I have no more trouble from that pair. Soon as it's possible to travel, I want them on their way over the passes and out of this country. Don't give them the idea they're getting away with anything!"

Bannister didn't answer, for a moment. Inwardly he thought, so you're loading it onto the marshal's office! Instead of making an effort yourself, you turn them loose on society and expect the law to control them. . . .

It was damned hard to feel much sympathy for this man, in spite of the tragic loss that had befallen him. Bannister doubted that it had really changed or softened him. Hard to see how a fellow like Grady Sullivan could continue to serve such an employer, and with such blind loyalty.

But none of this was Jim Bannister's concern. He shrugged. "All right, Pauling," he said. "If you're sure that's what you want," he pulled on the hat he had removed when he entered the room, "I'll see that it's done. . . ."

CHAPTER VI

Jim Bannister left Tepee in a savage mood, and in no hurry to get back to Morgantown and the distasteful business of freeing his prisoners. It would not hurt Tate Pauling any, but he knew that having that pair loose would be like placing a cocked sixgun at his own back.

To settle his anger, and to enjoy for a little longer the pleasure of an hour or so alone and with no demands on him, he chose a longer return route by crossing the creek at a fording where the ice crackled and broke under the hoofs of his horse.

West of the creek the valley floor was more frequently broken by spurs thrown out from the high enclosing wall; the grass was generally poorer, and this was where Tate Pauling's smaller neighbors ran their herds and had their home ranches. They had come in and taken the leavings, with no challenge from Tate Pauling because he didn't want it himself. Afterward it was only human, perhaps, for them to look across to the choice acres of deeded land belonging to Tepee—as extensive as all their own outfits combined—and resent what they saw.

Tate Pauling's arrogance and spiteful nature merely added an unnecessary touch to their jealousy.

Bannister soon got into broken range, thinly timbered, with the hollows choked with drifts while the hilltops were swept bare by the scouring winds; there the road ruts were frozen to iron and gave back the beat of a horse's hoofs with a ring and shock that its rider could almost feel. It was from one of these crests that Bannister saw something that made him pull up, in thoughtful interest.

Three riders—a couple of them together, and the third some quarter mile to the rear—were moving at an easy pace across a snow-covered flat, along a secondary wagon road. Now the first pair, as though only just becoming aware of someone behind them, halted and half-turned their horses to wait. The third overtook them and hands were raised in greeting.

They appeared to converse for a moment, while their horses stepped around impatiently and kicked up puffs of ground snow for the winter sun to turn to sparkling diamonds. Presently the three rode on again, in a tight single file.

By this time Bannister had his saddle bag open and was adjusting a pair of field glasses. They could not tell him enough to identify positively either the riders, in their heavy winter clothing, or the shaggy-coated horses. But one of the men looked a good deal like Dave Pitts, and he thought he recognized a Cloverleaf brand on the piebald animal in the lead. That brand belonged to Bart Reiner, another of the small valley ranchers.

He swung the glasses ahead, then, to pick up the low-lying cluster of buildings that appeared to be their goal. He didn't know the valley well, but he judged that would have to be Gil Rickman's Bear Paw headquarters.

He lowered the glasses, frowning. Rickman appeared to have company coming—and likely it was more than a coincidence that would bring his neighbors converging on him in this fashion, at the same hour of the same wintry Sunday afternoon.

To Jim Bannister it had the looks of a meeting of some kind, deliberately called and for a purpose. And while it might be no concern of the marshal's office, on the heels of yesterday evening—and Grady Sullivan's warning of serious trouble in the making—he became conscious of a growing and uneasy suspicion.

His mind quickly made up, he stepped down on frozen earth that shocked his heels with its hardness, put away the glasses and took out a pair of pliers. Lifting the bay's off rear hoof, he deliberately pried out the nails, pulled off the worn shoe and flung it away into a clump of naked brush. Afterward, mounted again, he rode ahead toward the juncture with the turnoff where the fresh tracks of a number of horses preceded him.

Rickman, he knew, was a bachelor; and Bear Paw turned

51

out to be about what he had imagined. The contrast with Tate Pauling's headquarters was total.

Tucked into a cramped hollow with a hogback ridge behind it, the place boasted a main house that was little more than a log shanty for housing the owner and his two-man crew, and a scatter of additional sheds with a single stock corral. Smoke rose from a mud chimney. There was an unkempt and slovenly air about the whole layout.

A brindle hound, chained to a stake driven into the ground, raised a challenge as Bannister came up. There was no one in sight in the yard, but a half dozen horses were tied to the corral fence; all under saddle and all bearing different valley brands. Among them he noticed one rawboned brown gelding, bearing a patched and well-worn rig which he recognized as the property of the hapless Ira Stiegel. Bannister looked at the horses and wondered.

Meanwhile the hound, who had already seen too many visitors for one day, was keeping up its hysterical performance, sweeping back and forth in a semicircle at the end of its chain and frantically tearing up the snow.

Abruptly, the door of the house was thrown open, and Gil Rickman himself stepped out with an angry yell and flung a stick of stove wood at the dog. As it subsided, he turned to Bannister. A suspicious frown puckered the narrow, bitter eyes. "Marshal Bryan," he said.

Bannister nodded. "Hope I'm not interrupting anything."

It was half a question but the other man wouldn't answer it. He demanded sullenly, "You got business with me, maybe?"

"Not exactly." Bannister was dismounting as he spoke. "It's the bay, here—he threw an iron, somewhere back along the pike. Your spread was handiest, so I rode in. Thought maybe I could replace it."

Rickman continued to stare belligerently. He seemed to be testing the explanation, trying to decide if he was satisfied with it. Other men showed now in the doorway, behind the rancher, crowding for a look at what was going on in the yard. Bannister glimpsed Ira Stiegel's sad, narrow face, with its slanting cheekbones and chopped-off yellow straggle of beard.

A trifle reluctantly, he thought, the Bear Paw owner said, "If you want to take your animal around back, you'll find everything you need in the shed. Help yourself."

"Thanks. Don't let me interrupt whatever you're doing."

Rickman shrugged. "Just a few of the boys, dropped by for—" he paused, almost imperceptibly "—for a round of poker."

Bannister nodded and led his animal around the side of the house, with Rickman still staring after him in the hard, thin sunlight. The smithy was an open-faced shed; here there were anvil and tools, charcoal for the forge, a gunny sack containing horseshoes—and, also, a fair view over a good part of the yard.

He went directly to work, but all the time remaining alert to anything that took place within his range of vision. In the time it took to select a shoe, scrape the bay's hoof and get a fire going with the aid of patched leather bellows, two more riders had drifted in.

As he worked the bellows, turning the shoe in the coals, Bannister watched them add their horses to the tiepole along the corral fence, and disappear into the house. It was a meeting, no doubt of that; but, so far, he had no hint as to the nature of it. Curiosity beat higher in him with every passing minute.

Warming to his work, Bannister had peeled out of his Windbreaker and hung it on a nail. He was at the anvil, shaping the glowing metal with a practiced rhythm of hammer strokes, when Gil Rickman left his guests and came out to lean his shoulders against the roof prop while, with folded arms, he watched Bannister at work. He had a pipe clamped between his hard jaws; the foul smell of the cheap shag that he used reached Bannister from time to time, even above that of the forge and heating iron.

To Bannister it was clear the man was nervous and suspicious, not fully convinced either by the missing shoe, or by the fact that it could not have waited until the owner of the bay reached town. Rickman asked suddenly, "You got business of some kind, out in the valley?"

"I had to have a talk with Tate Pauling."

"Was he sober enough?" Rickman gave a sneering laugh.

53

Bannister ignored the remark and, after a moment, the other demanded bluntly, "Were you talking about us, here on this side of the creek?"

"Should we have been?"

Glancing across a shoulder he saw the man's angry shrug. "How the hell would I know? All that wild talk Sullivan was throwing around last night—I thought you might even have begun taking it seriously."

"This was a different matter entirely," Jim Bannister said and closed the subject. He laid aside the hammer, used the tongs to thrust the shoe into the water butt and then tested the results against the bay's hoof; afterward he put it back into the coals and worked the bellows handle again.

There were no more probing questions, but neither did Gil Rickman show any sign of leaving. He built a fog of smoke from his foul-smelling pipe, while the bitter eyes in that odd, wedge-shaped face of his watched Bannister's every move—in itself a routine performance—that he could scarcely have found all that interesting. All too clearly he was simply impatient for Bannister to finish and be on his way, and lacked the subtlety to keep it from being obvious.

The tall man pretended not to notice.

The job was, at last, done. Bannister released the gelding's hind leg that he had held clamped between his thighs, set the hoof down and straightened, tossing the hammer and a couple of unused nails onto a bench. He put his hands against the small of his back to stretch the muscles, said, "That's that. Can I pay you for the shoe?" The other curtly shook his head. "Well—thanks a lot."

"Any time."

Rickman followed him as he led the bay out from under the shed roof; hands in hip pockets, pipe in mouth, he watched the tall man check his handiwork, then gather the reins and swing astride. A frigid wind was strengthening, blowing its breath along the earth. "Getting colder," Gil Rickman said, around the pipe stem. "Too cold to snow, I reckon."

Bannister worked at the fastenings of his Windbreaker. "This time of year, who can say?"

So, on an exchange of trivialities, he took his leave; but

he was sure there had been something real hidden beneath the banal surface. At a little distance he pulled rein and half-turned the bay for a look behind him, squinting at the glare the heatless winter sun put on the hoof-chopped freeze of mud and snow that was the Rear Paw yard.

Rickman was heading for the shack with a reaching and purposeful stride, while the line-up of saddled horses along the corral fence stomped and blew steam from their nostrils. Through the window he could vaguely make out the dark shapes of men moving around inside.

Bannister's mouth was a trifle grim as he settled into leather and gave the bay a kick. He'd completely failed in his purpose of trying to get some clue—perhaps from a carelessly dropped word or two—as to just what was going on here this afternoon. But whatever, he knew for damn sure it was no poker game. And he didn't like it.

Bert Dakins, facing an afternoon in charge of both jail and prisoners, did so with less than real enthusiasm. He couldn't have explained, but there was something about that pair in the cellblock—even disarmed and securely put away—that troubled him badly.

It was actually very seldom he had ever had a prisoner to guard, and then nothing more than a cowpuncher who had taken on too much liquor in celebrating a night on the town, and who had been meekly contrite and easily bullied when he came to in a cell, the morning after. Never had he seen anything like this pair of prisoners.

Clausen, the redhead, had a foul tongue and a slashing, wicked insolence of manner that he was completely unable to match and which kept him off balance, so that he felt more like a servant running errands than a custodian of helpless prisoners.

But it was the other one—Billy Ide, with the silent, cold stare and the expressionless pale face marked by the ugly knife scar—that he positively recoiled from, somehow recalling the evil reptilian head of a rattlesnake he had once nearly stumbled upon when scrambling among some sunsmitten rocks as a kid.

Billy Ide merely sat on his bunk and watched him

silently, while Virg Clausen cursed and raged; but it was this silent watching that unnerved Dakins the most.

Dakins had spent some of the morning out back, working with axe and saw on that snag of dead pine that Bryan had hauled down. It was not a job at which he had any skill and he barked up the knuckles of both hands, cursing and complaining to himself the entire time; but he managed to knock up a modest quantity of firewood for the two stoves.

About the time he finished, the man from the hotel dining room came over bearing the prisoners' their second meal of the day. Dakins unlocked the cell for him with a key on his belt ring and stood by, sixgun in hand, while the tin plates of food were put inside and the remains of breakfast collected. He said nothing to Clausen's angry threats, and carefully avoided even looking at the silent figure on the other bunk.

He ate his own dinner, then, hunched at the desk in the office, snuffling and coughing and more certain every moment that he had caught cold from working himself into a sweat out there in the raw winter weather. When a peremptory shout summoned him to the cell block he heaved up with a groan and a curse, his meal unfinished, and went back there.

Billy Ide was standing at the tiny barred window, with his back turned. It was the redhead, Clausen, who gave him a scowl and said harshly, "It's getting cold in here again. Do something about it, will you?"

The fire in the stove was down to sullen coals. Muttering, Dakins laid on fresh wood and then opened the draft full, and in a moment had flames roaring in the flue, showing through the joints. Deliberately he let the pipe start to turn cherry red, where it bent to pierce the wall, before he closed it off with an angry twist of the damper.

Clausen had watched all this casually, leaning his forearms on a crosspiece of the metal door with wrists dangling outside the bars. Now as Dakins plodded back toward the office, the redhead saw his martyred expression and said, grinning, "Your boss lays the work on you, does he?"

That halted Dakins, his narrow ferret's face coloring. "Bryan? He ain't my boss!"

56

"He appears to think so."

"Only man has a right to give me orders," the jailer declared, stung, "is old Sam White. After all the years I put in, if there was any justice it should be me serving as acting marshal, now that Sam's laid up."

"You know, I been wondering about that." Virg Clausen canted his head and bleak winter light, through the window, shone on a reddish stubble of unshaved whiskers. "This is a pretty dead burg. No reason they need such a tough bastard to run it."

Bert Dakins snorted. "Town marshal here ain't much more'n a night watchman—at least, in the winter. Generally, about half the merchants shut down and leave Morgantown before the passes close, and turn things over to the marshal's office to keep an eye on for them. I wouldn't be surprised but what there's a spare key to every business house in town, accumulated in that desk in the other room. And it sure don't take any gunman just to go around checking doors."

"And just who the hell is this tough nobody Sam White's gone and shoved into the job? From all I hear, ain't a soul in Morgantown knows where he come from, or anything about him."

"For a fact!" exclaimed Bert Dakins, warming to a favorite subject. "Sam and me jumped his camp one night last fall, back in the hills, when he was out with a posse hunting that Luke Harbord fellow we thought had killed the Pauling girl. Well, before anyone could explain how he'd been mistook for someone else, this Bryan started shooting and he put a bullet into Sam's leg. That's how come Sam is laid up, right now—it was Bryan himself that shot him!"

Billy Ide had drifted over from the window to hear this tale. For once, so engrossed was Dakins with his own grievances and with finding a sympathetic ear to hear them, that he almost forgot his terror of the blond man. Now the prisoners exchanged a look and Billy Ide remarked quietly, "Sounds like an itchy trigger finger, don't it?"

Clausen nodded soberly, his eyes thoughtfully narrowed. "A strange pick, to fill the marshal's job. . . ." He asked

Dakins, "You dead certain him and White was all that much strangers?"

"How do you mean?"

"I'm just wondering if this Bryan might have been using some kind of a lever on the old man. . . ."

"*Blackmail?*" Dakins stared at him; as though horrified. But then a knowing look descended upon his narrow face; he glanced quickly over his shoulder as he drew nearer to the bars. His voice became conspiratorial.

"By God!" he said. "There *is* something funny, there! From the very first, I've had kind of a hunch there was something they knew and wasn't spreading. And I ain't the only one, either. I've heard people talk. It does seem mighty peculiar—"

The words died on his tongue. His eyes popped; his tongue clove to the roof of a mouth suddenly gone dry. Slowly—almost as though his neck needed oiling—he lowered his head by jerky degrees and from the corners of his eyes looked down at the gun that had slid out of his holster to be shoved, hard, into his ribs. He looked at the hand, with the red fur matting it, thrust between the bars; he shuddered violently, with terror and humiliation for the way he had been tricked and thrown off his guard. Then he forced his eyes to lift and meet Virg Clausen's stare.

"You're doing just fine," the redhead said with mocking gentleness. "Steady, now, and you won't get hurt.

"Unlock the door!"

Bert Dakins tried to protest, but no sound came past his lips. Eyes still on Clausen's, he fumbled at his belt, found the key ring and attempted to fit the key into the lock. But his fingers shook so that Billy Ide cursed and, slipping his own hand through the bars, took the key away from him. The lock clicked open; Dakins was flung back, hard, against the opposite wall as the iron door burst open in his face.

Paying him no further attention, the escaping prisoners were already hurrying down the corridor, pulling on coats and hats as they went.

Dakins never knew where he found the courage to will strength into his shaking knees. But, somehow, a moment

58

later he was in the office doorway and there he halted, clinging to the door frame for support.

The gunbelts and weapons that had been taken off the prisoners the previous night were hanging on the pegs of a wall rack, each tagged with its owner's name; now Virg Clausen was taking them down. He tossed Billy Ide's gun to him, and set to work buckling his own rig about his waist. The sixshooter he had taken from Bert Dakins lay discarded on the desk.

The jailer found his voice; it sounded desperately foreign in his own ears. "You just can't do this!" he cried hoarsely. "You know you'll never make it out of town. . . ."

"Who said anything about leaving?" Virg Clausen retorted, across his shoulder. "There's no place to go, unless a man wants to tackle the passes. And I reckon we're in no hurry to do that." A last hitch at his gunbelt settled it to his liking, and now he drew his rubber-handled sixgun and rocked open the loading mechanism, checked the shells. Satisfied, he nodded and shoved the gun back into holster.

Billy Ide was already at the street door; the blond man opened it a crack, cast a look into the street. As cold air swept into the room, Virg Clausen turned back for one last detail. He strode heavily toward Bert Dakins, who drew back a little before his advance, and laid the point of a forefinger against the jailer's narrow chest. "I got a message for your friend Bryan. Make sure you give it to him."

"All right."

"We promised that yellow-headed bastard we'd have things to settle with him, for what happened last night. Well, you can tell him we're ready when *he* is. If he's got the nerve to try his luck a second time, all he has to do is come looking. He'll find us waiting!"

Bert Dakins swallowed, nodding. Apparently satisfied with that, Virg Clausen swung about and followed his partner from the jail.

CHAPTER VII

Jim Bannister, returning from his afternoon's ride up-valley, felt an acute and instant awareness of something wrong within five minutes of entering Morgantown. It reached him first when a pair of townsmen saw him and halted in mid-stride. Instantly one turned back at a spirited run along the single line of buildings, to disappear into the hotel lobby with all the manner of one who relayed an expected message.

Puzzled, Bannister rode on, angling toward the jail where he swung down and tied. He looked toward the hotel as he did so, and saw a half dozen men come trooping out onto the veranda to cluster there, staring in his direction. It came strongly home to him, then, that the whole town had been waiting for his return. Something must have happened while he was gone.

Deliberately he kicked mud and snow from his boots against the door sill and walked inside, undoing the fastenings of his blanket coat. When he saw Bert Dakins, huddled in the chair behind the desk, one look at the man's face confirmed all his guesses. He dropped his hand from the coat's fastenings, and stood eyeing the jailer coldly.

"All right," he said. "Let's hear it."

Dakins lifted a face that looked sick. He had the air of a trapped animal. His eyes tried to meet Bannister's but then they slid away, as though drawn involuntarily toward the cell-block doorway. Bannister caught the direction of his glance; it took him across the office floor, and through the bars he saw the empty cell with its door standing open. He wheeled about, and his face was like iron.

He said, too quietly, "I thought I left you with a couple of prisoners. . . ."

Bert Dakins touched tongue to dry lips, and his whole whole body shook as he quailed before the tall man's look. "I—I'm afraid they got loose, Bryan."

"How?" Bannister snapped. "How could they possibly?"

"They tricked me. They took my gun." The jailer's sweating face writhed in a grimace. "I still don't know how they managed. Honest to God, Bryan—"

Bannister's look silenced him. "So you let them have your gun. . . ." A glance at the wall pegs showed him that the weapons he had taken from Clausen and Ide were missing. He took a breath. "How long ago was this?"

"Couple hours. Oh, they ain't left town," the man added quickly. "Said they hadn't no aim of leaving. They're waiting to see if you—if we want to try and take them a second time." Dakins came to his feet, almost babbling. "I been doing some figuring. They're waiting up at the Dutchman's. Now, if we was just to get a bunch of the boys to go with us—"

"No." The tall man shook his head. "This is meant as a personal challenge," he said heavily. "For me alone, not for a bunch of boys—who wouldn't help, anyway. Now that it's happened, it's in my lap and in no one else's—certainly not in yours."

Dakins's voice held a shaky hint of near-hysteria. "Bryan, I wouldn't want anyone thinking I'm *afraid* of that pair! I tell you, they tricked me. It could have happened to anybody!"

A stale disgust rimmed Bannister's voice. "My horse is outside. Unsaddle him and put him in the shed."

Silenced, Bert Dakins nodded. "Right away," he muttered. He grabbed up hat and coat and scurried out, as though relieved to escape.

Alone, Jim Bannister swore. He took an angry tour of the jail office, and feeling pain in his knife-slashed left palm glanced down to see that the bandaged hand was tightly clenched. He shook his head at that, and with a movement of his broad shoulders forced himself to ease off his irritation and angry tension.

Because of the incompetence of Bert Dakins, a nasty piece of work had been dumped unnecessarily into his lap; but, there was nothing for it.

A pot of much-boiled coffee stood on the back of the woodburner; he found a tin cup, poured himself a shot of the strong black brew, and drank it while he considered. Afterward he drew his sixgun and was checking the loads when, upon the door's opening, he glanced up expecting to see Dakins returned from his chore of unsaddling the bay. Instead Stella Harbord closed the door and faced Bannister with an expression of fright and consternation.

Her eyes touched the gun in his hands. She said in a toneless voice, "You're going to the Dutchman's. . . ."

"I've got no choice," he said.

"You'll be killed! The whole town knows it, and they'll just stand by and watch it happen."

Bannister clicked the cylinder of the sixgun into place, slipped the weapon into his holster. Then he picked up the hat he had laid on the desk, and walked over to the door. "A man can't always pick the rules the game must be played by," he said solemnly. "Once the hand is dealt, he plays it the best he can."

"But it's for nothing, Jim!" she exclaimed. "Nothing at all. And—I don't want you killed!"

He looked down at her, seeing the anxious concern in her eyes, the lift of her breast on troubled breathing. "Stella—" he said, and touched her shoulder. And then, with a single movement, his arm was moving about her and she came against him. Her lips came up, searching for his own; their kiss was a blind and hungry meeting.

When he released her they stood close and looked at one another with eyes that held new meaning. At last Jim Bannister spoke gruffly. "I suppose we both knew this was coming, Stella. I blame myself. I shouldn't have let it happen."

"Why?" she challenged, clear-eyed and direct. "Because of Luke? And your Marjorie?"

"No, not because of that. We can't carry the dead past around with us forever. But, I'm no one for you to become interested in! A man without a future—"

She shook her head, and her lips trembled on a smile. "You think I haven't told myself that? And do you suppose it makes any difference?" Her expression changed. Her hand came up to tighten on his sleeve. "But—does it make any difference to *you,* Jim? Maybe now, for my sake if not for your own—"

"I'll back away from this business waiting for me at the Dutchman's? I'm sorry," he said firmly. "I *wish* I could! I wish I could be that much less of a man. It's not just because of that pair of trash," he went on. "There's an element in this town that would be happy to see me take a fall. If I should try to side-step this time, I might as well throw in my badge—I wouldn't be able to hold up my head in Morgantown again. . . ."

Her hand fell from his arm. She made no move to stop him as he opened the door and stepped out into the chill afternoon.

Outside, Bannister drew on his hat, filled his lungs with the crisp winter air, moved his shoulders to settle the hang of his blanket coat. He stood a moment looking upstreet toward the big log building that housed the Dutchman's— still the town's chief saloon—a relic of palmier days. As he turned and started in that direction he seemed to feel the weight of a hundred watching eyes.

His mind was only halfway tuned to the thing that awaited him there; instead, he thought of that moment with Stella—the taste of her mouth, the feel of her in his arms, the look in her eyes as the thing that had been so long unspoken between them finally and explosively came into the open—all this still dominated and colored all his thoughts.

To overcome it he tried now to narrow and focus his attention on immediate sensory impressions: The grind of the frozen mud beneath his deliberately pacing boots, the raw touch of the wind against his face, and the sound of it booming along the gulch where Morgantown clung to its raw foundations.

This act of will carried him the rest of the distance, and when he turned and climbed the split-log steps to the saloon porch his nerves were keenly alert, his attention sharpened.

He paused a moment to open the blanket coat and push the skirt of it back, clearing the holstered gunbutt. Then he turned the knob of the steamed-over glass door, and stepped

63

inside. At once every sound in the room sheared off as abruptly as if an axe blade had fallen.

In its day, and with a different owner, the Dutchman's had been as ornate as any gold camp west of Denver could have boasted. Even now its interior was garish with gilded plaster and oil paintings of nudes and a glittering back bar, though much of the gold paint had peeled.

Holding his ground, Bannister looked around and thought that most of the male population of Morgantown must be concentrated here, but they did not do much to fill a room this size.

Every head was turned toward the door.

Billy Ide stood alone at the bar with a bottle and half-filled whiskey glass in front of him. Some little distance away, at a round-topped table, redheaded Virg Clausen sat—also alone—and dealt himself a spread of solitaire. But drinking and cards were forgotten, now; Jim Bannister saw it was all set up and waiting for him.

As he took a step farther into the room, there was a sudden movement back against the walls—a scuff of boots and scrape of emptying chairs that quickly died away leaving the area before the bar deserted, except for the three central figures in the drama. And now Billy Ide slid a hand into his clothing and brought it out holding a glittering streak of metal.

So he had found himself another knife somewhere!

At sight of it Jim Bannister's jaw muscles bunched hard, but he would not let himself show fear; he kept going, deliberately.

Billy Ide laid his wrist lightly on the bar and watched him come, a cruel eagerness in his grin. Yonder, meanwhile, without moving from his chair, Virg Clausen had silently put down his deck of cards and let a hand drop from sight under the table's edge.

There was the painful silence of trapped, withheld breath in a score of throats, as Bannister came to a halt facing the man with the knife. He had the bar at his left elbow, his right side toward Clausen's table. It was impossible to face them both at once, from this angle, and he knew that was what

64

they had been maneuvering for when they took up their positions.

He gave no sign that he was aware of this. He leaned the point of his elbow on the wood and said, "You see, I got your message."

Even with the advantage of two against one, and with an audience that was plainly eager to see this tall stranger tested, Billy Ide seemed tensed and cautious. He had to tilt his head to face Bannister; he threw a glance at his partner, as though looking for a cue. "Yeah," he said gruffly. "Virg and me, we been wondering if you'd show. We'd just about given up waiting."

"I only now got in," Bannister assured him. "I came directly I'd been to the jail and learned what happened."

"That stupid Bert Dakins told you all about it, I reckon."

"He told me enough. I didn't need the details."

Hunting through the litter of shot glasses at his elbow, Bannister found a clean one. Quite deliberately he filled it from the bar bottle, but he made no immediate move to take his drink. Instead, twisting the glass in idle circles on the bartop, he put his level gaze on the man beside him.

He said, coldly, "Whatever you mean to do, let's get on with it. Unless of course you want to reconsider—it's not too late."

He put into the words a deliberate and studied contempt that did not get past Billy Ide. The blond man's eyes blinked, his lips parted on a sucked-in breath. Suddenly color rushed into his face and turned the knife scar livid. And with a cry of rage he lunged at Bannister, the blade rising in his fist.

Jim Bannister was ready. He took an unhurried step backward and let Billy Ide have the drink he'd poured—tumbler and all—squarely in the face. Ide went double, dropping the knife as he squalled in pain and clapped both hands to his burning eyes.

In the same moment Bannister, falling into a crouch, was scooping the gun from his holster twisting to bring it to bear on Virg Clausen. The redhead had been caught by surprise, likely not thinking his partner would be goaded into starting trouble before some prearranged signal could pass; he came blundering to his feet now, scattering cards and jarring the table in front of him as he dragged up the gun he had been holding in his lap.

Bannister's quick move toward the floor had for a moment robbed him of a target. Before Clausen had time to find it again, Bannister triggered deliberately. His shot plowed a groove across the table's green felt and made Clausen yell and scramble wildly backward, only to become tangled with his chair. By the time he had fought for and regained his balance, Bannister was already standing again and holding the redhead covered with his smoking gun.

"Empty your hand!" he ordered, into the ear-punishing echoes of that single shot.

Clausen, looking dazed and confused, blinked stupidly at the weapon he was holding; he opened his fingers and let it fall to the boards in front of him. Thereupon Jim Bannister turned to Billy Ide who was still pawing at his streaming, blinded eyes. The knife lay forgotten, and he had only to reach and pluck the gun from the blond man's holster and lay it on the bar.

It was over as quickly as that.

The crowd seemed as stunned as the pair he had disarmed. Even though the danger was clearly over they still hung back, no one speaking or moving yet. Behind the counter the bartender was backed against the mirror with his hands well in sight and a look of disbelief smeared across his sweating face. Bannister knew that Morgantown would not be finished talking about the thing that had happened here for a long time to come.

Having let a single searching look touch the rest of the scene, he turned again to his prisoners. He drew a breath and said, in heartfelt contempt, "You're certainly a fine lot of scum! A less patient man than me wouldn't put up with you!"

Virg Clausen had found his voice. He was shaken but he managed to put defiance into it. "You bastard! Your luck can't always be that good." And to his partner, who had lost all his icy aplomb and been reduced to sobbing and blaspheming soddenness, he added bitterly, "Shut up—you ain't hurt! The oldest trick in the world—and you let him do it to you! Thanks to you, we're headed back to jail!" He kicked aside the chair he had knocked over, came around the table toward the marshal with a sullen look on his face. "All right, damn you—let's go then!"

Bannister, favoring him with a level stare, slowly shook his head and saw a beginning puzzlement spread across the faces of both his prisoners. "I have news for you. Tate Pauling's withdrawn all charges, mainly because it isn't worth the bother taking you to court. I came back from his place this afternoon intending to turn you loose—with a warning that nobody wants to see you around here, once the passes open. Now, both of you, get out of my sight!"

Virg Clausen very nearly stammered. "You mean—you mean you knew that? And yet you let us go ahead and—"

"You had to have it this way," Bannister told him coolly, "so I obliged you. But if there's another time, I'll take no more nonsense off you. I hope that's clear!" He left it to sink in. About to turn away, he remembered and fished up a coin from his pocket, which he tossed upon the bar. "For the drink I spilled," he told the barkeep and got a stare for an answer.

The whole room seemed held, still, in the grip of astonishment. He knew they shared the vague resentment that most men—even honest ones—felt toward a law badge. They had expected to see this tall stranger taken for a fall and likely enough they were a little disappointed. For his part, Jim Bannister was not yet sure himself how it had turned out the way it did.

He shrugged, easing the tightness from his shoulders. He shoved the gun back into its holster and walked out of the saloon, and found Stella Harbord waiting on the sidewalk. There was incredulous relief in her tense white face as she saw him coming to her, whole and unharmed.

CHAPTER VIII

Morning mist hid the peaks, and Jim Bannister wondered if a new freight of unspilled snow waited to plague this high country. Climbing the zigzag flight of steps to banker Youngdahl's steep-roofed mansion, he reflected that the patience and sanity of Morgantown were already stretched fine by winter and could snap under the weight of any more. He remembered something someone had said to him: "This whole damn valley has got cabin fever!"

He squinted at a single spot of brightness that was the sun trying to burn its way through the greasy overcast, then mounted to the porch and gave a yank at the bell knob.

There was a considerable wait. He was about to ring again when the door was opened by Claude Youngdahl himself. The banker, in shirtsleeves but wearing a cravat and one of his elegant silk waistcoats, peered out suspiciously and with no immediate evidence of intending to throw the door wide enough to let him in. "Oh. It's you, Bryan," he said, his voice oddly loud. "You're earlier than I expected."

Irritation pulled at Bannister's brow and he answered curtly, "Your man said you wanted to see me right away."

The other simply shrugged. He had an abstracted manner, almost as though he were listening for some sound from within the house behind him; and Bannister thought suddenly: There's someone here, and he doesn't want me to know! A woman? He doubted it. The idea just did not fit with this bloodless young man, of the soft hands and the too-pale skin. Especially when there was scarcely any competition available, in storm-trapped Morgantown, for Claude Youngdahl's own sleek and glittering blond wife. . . .

The thoughts had scarcely crossed his mind when he heard, or else imagined, a tread of heavy footsteps that were muffled by thick carpeting and then cut off by the closing of a door somewhere at the rear of the house.

On the instant the banker's whole manner seemed to change; he stepped back throwing the door wide. "Come in—come in," he said in a brusk tone. "It's a raw day. Thought I'd stay home, this morning—catch up on some work where I can do it undisturbed." He ushered his guest inside, the tall man pulling off his hat as he passed through the archway—puzzled by all this and feeling, as always, out of place here.

Though he knew little of such things, Bannister was struck by a contrast between this elegantly furnished living room and the crude masculinity of the one he had seen at Tepee.

So far as he could tell, Tate Pauling might have spent the same amount of money; vaguely, he supposed what made the difference was the thing called taste. A log was blazing in the fireplace, sparks snapping and pouring up the chimney. The round mahogany table where, two days ago, he had watched a poker game in progress, was now piled with ledgers and spread-out working papers covered with figures.

And there was something else.

In the moment of entering, it hit him so strongly that he halted involuntarily for an instant on the threshold. He remembered that the man beside him was not a smoker; yet certainly the tang of cheap pipe tobacco was here, an elusive whiff of it that seemed oddly familiar and that he felt he was on the verge of recognizing until the pungent odor of the burning pine log covered and blotted it out.

Nevertheless, he was ready now to take oath that someone who had been in this room had left it hurriedly— and probably the house as well, by a rear door.

At least Youngdahl's initially furtive manner had vanished and he seemed at ease again. He poured a couple of drinks from the cut-glass decanter, handed one glass to his guest and took the other to the table at which he seated himself with one arm hooked across the back of his chair.

Bannister did not wait to be invited, but let himself down in a comfortable wing chair near the fire. He set his own drink aside untasted and waited for the banker to explain his summons.

69

Instead Youngdahl began by saying, "I understand Tate Pauling had himself an accident a couple of evenings ago."

"You could call it that."

"What I heard was, a couple of toughs worked him over." Youngdahl looked into his glass, and drank. "Have you seen him?" He watched Bannister's nod, above the tumbler's rim. "Was the old pirate hurt bad?"

"No. He appears to be doing all right."

"The good fortune of fools and drunkards," the other said, with a shake of the head. "Would you believe it, he's one man who's never yet set foot inside my bank. I don't know the reason, but I've had practically no dealings with him at all. He refuses to let me handle his money; if he ever had call to make a loan he'd likely as not go outside—to Denver, or somewhere. A strange man. . . ."

Bannister, with a shrewd look at the other's pale face, thought: He's one you can't see any way to put your hooks into. I don't reckon you like that!

Youngdahl set aside his glass. "And this Clausen and Ide. This was the same tough pair you had your run-in with at the Dutchman's yesterday?"

"So you heard about that, too?"

"I've heard little else! Don't you know better than to take risks with men of that stripe? You could have found a charge of some sort. Disturbing the peace . . . anything. You're going to regret you left them loose."

"It's possible. Still, a lawman can't use the jail as a place to put his personal enemies. That can only make him look like a coward."

"I hardly think anyone considers you a coward, Bryan. Not after yesterday." Youngdahl cocked his head, pursing the full, moist lips as he considered the big man seated by the fire. He said suddenly, "I was wondering if you'd thought any more about the proposition that was made to you in this room, on Saturday. . . ."

Bannister stiffened, in quick irritation. "If you mean, that I replace Sam White—there's nothing to think about. I told you then, I wouldn't be interested."

"I know you did," the other agreed blandly. "But you've

70

had time to reconsider; and so have I. After yesterday, you look considerably more valuable. Perhaps, worth a bonus."

"Oh? What sort of bonus?"

The man's soft fingers fluttered a silent rhythm on the table top as he considered Bannister. "I don't think you're a fool, and neither am I. Since there's no one to overhear us, I'm willing to say I'd consider it an investment if I were to offer the right man a little something extra, in addition to his regular salary . . . from my own pocket, that is. A hundred a month, perhaps. Would that interest you?"

Bannister's lids came down, narrowing the stare of his pale blue eyes. Lips stiff, he said carefully, "And you'd expect for your hundred—?"

"Let's call it cooperation," the other answered blandly. "I don't think I need to spell it out."

"No, I guess not." For a moment, as the log shifted and settled in its own charred ashes, putting a rich wash of light over the room's paneled walls and a roar of fire up the throat of the chimney, Jim Bannister met the banker's level gaze. Then, deliberately, he picked his hat off the carpet where he had laid it and swung to his feet.

"If this is what you wanted to see me about, you've wasted your time—and mine, too. There isn't one thing about your proposition that could possibly interest me! And I got other things to do, besides running up and down that hill to tell you so!"

Though the man didn't move, a quick light of anger heated the sharp black eyes, then hardened, and Claude Youngdahl's mouth took on firmness. "Are you certain of that—Bryan? Or whatever your name really is. . . ."

Bannister waited. The banker leaned forward suddenly, intensely.

"You don't honestly think I'm taken in by you? A man of your potential doesn't bury himself in a place like this and in such a thankless job without some good reason. I ask myself what that reason could be."

"Do you also ask yourself," Bannister retorted, unable to keep the anger from his voice, "what business it is of yours?"

71

"Of course it's my business!" the other chided him. "Both as a citizen and as a member of the council that was prevailed on to hire you!"

"When you hired me you must have thought you had good reason."

"My reasons were my own. . . . Just for the argument, let's suppose your name isn't Bryan. What it actually might be doesn't interest me in the least. To me, the important thing is that you're tough; you've got a gun, and evidently you aren't afraid to use it. I've been looking for a man like that.

"Now that Tate Pauling's day is up, I make no empty boast when I tell you I'm on my way to becoming a power in Morgan Valley—and a good deal sooner than anyone around here might expect. And the man who helps me get what I'm after will share the benefits, including full protection against anyone—anyone at all—who might show up and try to make trouble for something that happened before he came here. . . ."

"Are you finished?" Jim Bannister said, patiently. "Because I'm not for sale to you, at any price. Whatever it is you're trying to get, you'll have to get it without me or my gun!"

Claude Youngdahl sat and looked up at the tall man, for a long minute. Then, very slightly, he shrugged. His voice was quiet but the anger was still there, coloring it and turning his black eyes dangerous.

"Very well. If that's your choice, we won't discuss it again. But do one single thing to interfere with me, and you're going to be very, very sorry. That's a promise!"

"You take a step outside the law," Jim Bannister snapped, "and we'll see!" He pulled on his hat, turned, and walked out of that room and out of the house, letting the heavy door slam hard behind him.

Outside, with the chill wind to damp his anger, he told himself that it might have been smarter to have appeared to go along with Youngdahl, at least long enough to let the banker tip his hand by revealing whatever he would of the devious game he was playing. But, that went too hard against the grain—it was more pretense than Bannister was capable of, no matter how much it might have aided him in the complex and difficult job he had to do.

He was descending the twisting flights of wooden steps when an unexpected stab of memory all at once cleared away a mystery that had been puzzling him; it struck him so hard it brought him to a sudden halt, his eyes narrowing. That teasingly familiar hint of cheap tobacco, in Youngdahl's parlor—he knew now where he had encountered it before.

A picture of the blacksmith shed at Rickman's rose to him: The forge, the horseshoeing, and Gil Rickman looking on with a drift of foul blue smoke from his pipe building about him. No question about it, that was the memory that had been nagging at him.

Of course it might mean nothing. There could not be many brands of cheap tobacco to be had at the little stores there in the gulch, and others than Gil Rickman probably used the kind he favored. Moreover, there were a dozen reasons why he could have had business with someone to whom, like most of the valley, he was probably in debt.

But supposing it *was* Rickman, then why the secrecy? Why Youngdahl's evasiveness, when he deliberately held Bannister at the door until his previous caller—whoever it was—had had a chance to get out of the house, unseen?

The whole thing was most peculiar. And for that reason it troubled him. . . .

This day—Monday—dragged out. A day that was, for Jim Bannister, filled with minor irritations, haunted somehow by a sense of unrest and of pending events. He spent it mostly at paper work in his office, with the moody Bert Dakins—snuffling and complaining of a cold in the head—for company.

He did not go near Sam White's place. Without more than half admitting it to himself, Bannister knew he was avoiding Stella. He needed time to think, and so did she, after yesterday's unsettling revelation of their feeling for each other. Whatever happened next, they must pick their way carefully—both of them with eyes open to the predicament in which they now found themselves. . . .

73

There was some snow toward noon, a few scattered flakes in the air at any one time, that spiraled down from the gray overcast and were whipped about by the wind along the gulch. Then even this ended, and just as evening fell the clouds broke, the sky cleared.

Night came on cold and sparkling; but when, at midnight, Bannister went out for a last round of the village, putting Morgantown to bed, the night seemed surprisingly mild. The air had a new feel to it; the wind lacked its cutting edge. Perhaps this was actually it—a promise of the thaw for which this country was waiting.

It had been a quiet evening, without disturbances. At the Dutchman's, a single listless poker game at a back table under a harp lamp seemed on the verge of breaking up, and the bartender was putting away his liquor stock. A somnolent hush lay upon the town, and Bannister's own boots made almost the only sound as he walked his deliberate, patient beat.

He had no idea as to the whereabouts of Virg Clausen or Billy Ide. They were still around: He had reports of them, spending their time in a cheap saloon toward the lower end of the gulch, but seemingly they were staying out of his way. In some ways he preferred an enemy to keep in the open. A man walking alone in the night was all too conscious of the opportunities for an enemy to lay an ambush.

Wary but deliberate, he went about his business.

The last building at this upward end of the street was a general store, locked and boarded while its owner chose to spend the winter outside. Bannister tried the padlock on the main door, found all in order, and following the planks laid along the side of the building went around to check the back.

The rear of these main-street buildings sat close against a rock and clay embankment that rose steeply to another straggle of shacks and houses on a level just above. Back here the shadows were dense, broken only by dim starlight and the yellow square of shaded windowlight that marked Lloyd Canby's bachelor quarters in the rear of his store.

Passing behind Canby's to reach the building just beyond, Bannister picked a way among boxes and barrels of trash. As he came abreast of that lighted window, a half-submerged and nagging thought suddenly took shape unbidden: Virg Clausen, or Billy Ide, or anyone else who might have bothered to learn the timetable of his nightly rounds would have a perfect target when he moved across that square of lamplight.

The notion struck home so forcibly that he actually halted in his tracks. It was a move of pure instinct, and it very likely saved his life. He saw the smear of purple muzzle-flame above him; the revolver's flat crack, bouncing off rock faces and the lift of building walls, mingled with the smash of glass as the window went out.

Fallen back against dark clapboards, Jim Bannister fumbled out his own gun and, in the same instinctive moment, swung it up and let his thumb slide off the hammer flange, targeting the after-image. His shot was too hasty, but afterward he caught a brief sound of footsteps pounding hollowly on wood.

That placed his ambusher.

A crooked flight of steps climbed the bank a few yards ahead of him, and it was there the would-be killer had taken up his post. Now he was fleeing.

Anger sent Bannister in pursuit. He ducked below the level of the window, came up running. On reaching the bottom of the steps, he took them two at a time. Halfway up, his boot struck a patch of ice and he would have been thrown flat, except for a hand that caught the rickety railing and pulled him on.

Then he was on the upper level, with the scattered lights of main street below him and the mesh of stars overhead. He could hear the town coming awake around him now —doors and windows slamming open, voices shouting questions and, somewhere just ahead, a sound of running footsteps.

Bannister pressed his man hard, determined to stop him. He felt he was gaining; surely he should be getting some glimpse of the fugitive, against the dim background of piled-up snow. Then, suddenly, he did get it—almost too late. Either convinced he could not escape, or still bent on making a kill of it, the other had halted and turned. He was

75

down on one knee, waiting. Bannister plowed to a halt, caught the glimmer of a gun leveled at him, and fired without taking aim.

The shot was good.

The black shape of the ambusher spun and crumpled. With gun leveled and the echoes of the shot still in his ears, Jim Bannister slowly walked forward, and came to a stand over the motionless huddle that was the man he had downed.

His toe touched a gun, where it had fallen in the snow; he let that lie, and going down on one knee put a hand on the man's shoulder and rolled him over. He gave limply, as only a dead body does. With a numbness in him, Bannister dug out a match from his coat pocket and snapped it alight on a thumbnail.

Its thin yellow glow showed him staring eyes and a slack bearded face. The man was Reub Hodem, Morgantown's blacksmith—a fellow to whom he had spoken hardly a hundred words in all these months.

There could be no personal animosity, certainly—nothing to explain rationally what the man had tried to do. Yet he remembered, now, the black stare he had surprised on Hodem's face yesterday during church meeting; remembered how he had wondered at it, briefly, before dismissing it from his mind.

A nagging suspicion began to work at him.

Still holding the match, he shoved his sixshooter into the holster and laid a hand on the man's shirtfront, hoping without real hope to find a heartbeat, even though he knew the man was as dead as he would ever be.

It was thus that he discovered the fold of stiff paper in Hodem's shirt pocket. All at once he knew what it was, and his mouth went dry as he dug it out and shook open the folds. He sat there on his ankles and stared at his own face, on a duplicate of that reward dodger he had picked up from the floor of the jail office.

The match burned down to a black twist and he dropped it. Under his breath he said, "My guess was right!"

There was no other explanation. After all, Reub Hodem

76

had been one of the crowd that followed him and his prisoners into the jail. And so Hodem had picked up the poster there, had recognized it for the opportunity it was— if he could only somehow bring the thing off and collect the syndicate's reward money. He had watched, and bided his time; and tonight, at last, he had gotten up the nerve to make his try.

Bannister rubbed a palm across the cold flesh of his cheeks and thought: Who else did he tell? He'd been a bachelor, so there'd have been no wife to be taken into his confidence. Jim Bannister could only hope that greed had been stronger than the urge to gossip. . . .

After that he was straightening quickly to his feet, hastily shoving the paper from sight into a coat pocket, for other men were coming. They came from every direction, calling and shouting in excitement as the sound of the gunfight drew them. In another moment Bannister found himself surrounded. Lanterns, held high, shone in his face. He threw up a hand, irritably. "Get that light out of my eyes!" And into a babble of excited questions he explained, "I've had to shoot a man."

"It's Hodem! Reub Hodem!" A dozen voices took up the cry.

The crowd was swelling rapidly. Now Sid Noon, the liveryman who was a member of the council, shoved his way forward, with Mayor Ries tagging at his elbow. "What's happened here, Bryan?" he demanded. "By God, you better explain this!"

Bannister took a breath. "The man threw a bullet at me as I was crossing behind Canby's store. It missed and knocked out a window. I shot back and chased him up here; he was squaring off for another try when I drilled him. I didn't particularly aim to kill him. There's his gun," he added, pointing to where it lay on the ground beside the body. "You'll find a bullet fired from it."

Someone picked the weapon up and handed it to Sid Noon; someone else held a lantern while he rolled out the cylinder and sniffed at the chamber, all the time looking suspiciously at Bannister. He gave a grunt. "Now," he said, "maybe I'd better look at *your* gun!" Bannister hesitated, deeply reluctant, but he shrugged and, drawing the weapon from its holster, passed it over. "Two bullets fired," Noon reported. "To Hodem's one. . . ."

"Correct," Bannister said sharply, "but his was the first." He had caught sight of Lloyd Canby at the edge of the crowd now, and he appealed to the storekeeper. "You must have heard what happened. His bullet came from up here, and it broke your window."

Bareheaded, the storekeeper blinked at the lanternlight and exclaimed, anxiously, "I'm afraid I don't know anything. I was in the front of the store. And it all happened too fast—"

"Well, Bryan!" Sid Noon's cold stare was heavy with his dislike for this stranger who wore the marshal's badge. "It seems to be your word, and nothing else. What I'd like to hear is one good reason why Reub Hodem should want to murder you!"

They were all eyeing him, waiting; and suddenly Bannister knew he was stopped. Since he could not tell them the true reason, there was absolutely no way he could answer that question. He held his tongue, and saw the liveryman's craggy face settle into a look of grim satisfaction. Sid Noon nodded.

"It begins to add up! Here's a man wearing the marshal's badge, who's altogether too quick with a gun. Nobody would listen when I said, from the start, it was a bad mistake to hire somebody we didn't know. The kind of grandstand play he staged last night at the Dutchman's don't impress me in the least, because now we've seen the other side of the coin! Reub Hodem was no tough gunman. To us he was a fellow townsman, a man we've all known for—for a hell of a lot longer, certainly, than we've known this Jim Bryan! And now he lies dead, because Bryan saw something in the shadows and got rattled—and, thinking only of his own hide, began shooting without asking questions first.

"Maybe Reub Hodem did try to defend himself. If so, it did him little good. Against a professional—a hired killer—he never had a chance!"

78

Jim Bannister's hands were clenched. He saw the hostility growing solid in the faces about him as Sid Noon's arguments took effect; and all he could say, in a voice he fought to keep under control, was, "That's not the way it happened. You've got it wrong!"

"Have I?" the liveryman snapped. "It's the only answer that makes any sense! What's more, I say that the time has come to correct the mistake that never should have been made in the first place—even if it is too late to do Reub Hodem any good." He turned on Joe Ries, a sharp-featured little man with a wispy white mustache. "Joe, you're still mayor of this town, and I'm still a member of the council. I think our duty is clear."

"I think so too," said the druggist, with unwonted firmness. And he held out a palm to Bannister. "So, if you'll just unhook that badge, Mister Bryan—"

Bannister could not for an instant believe that he had heard right. But then, his face expressionless, he opened his coat, unpinned the badge from his shirt and laid it in Ries's palm. The latter said bleakly, "I suppose Bert Dakins can wear this for the time being—until the passes open and we have a chance to find us a new, permanent man to fill the marshal's job."

"Do I understand," Bannister snapped, "you mean to use this as your excuse to throw out Sam White? Is he being fired, along with me? He had nothing to do with what's happened here, tonight!"

"As I see it, he's more to blame than anyone else!" the mayor answered. "It was him talked us into hiring you. This seems as good a time as any to make the clean sweep of the marshal's office; that's more than overdue."

"You're dead right!" Sid Noon agreed; and Bannister knew then that the thing was settled. What he had been trying to prevent had at last come to pass. Sam White's job was gone—and he had Jim Bannister to thank for it.

The group moved to break up. Bannister spoke, as Sid Noon started to turn away with the others. "You've got my gun."

The liveryman's grizzled head swung toward him; his face

was a mask of stern dislike. But he shrugged, and with plain reluctance handed the weapon back. Jim Bannister slid it into his holster.

A long moment afterward he started walking down into the heart of the town, alone, following the bobbing lanterns and the men with their limply swaying burden.

CHAPTER IX

The whole morning seemed alive with a sound of running water—streams of melted water that sparkled in the bright sun as they channeled a way through black mud and from under old snowbanks. The sun, in a sky swept clear, had real warmth, and the wind that touched a man's skin felt different—warmer and dryer, as though it had blown in overnight with a purpose of eating up the deep drifts and bringing a first genuine, dramatic touch of spring to this besieged valley.

From the eaves of Sam White's little shack the melting icicles dripped bright lancets, sharp enough to make a man squint. They hung, an intermittant flashing curtain, in front of Bannister and Stella as they stood together on Sam's tiny porch in sober and troubled conversation.

"But what are you going to tell him?" the woman exclaimed, her anxious stare pinned on Bannister's.

He shrugged. "The truth. It won't be easy. I made a mistake, I think, not giving him at least some kind of warning before now that his job was in danger. But, I figured, what good would it do? His spirits were low enough without adding that."

She read his mood, and said quickly: "You don't blame yourself, certainly? You couldn't help what happened last night."

"That doesn't do Sam any good!" He drew off his hat, pushed his fingers through tawny hair, pulled the hat on

80

again. "Well, if he's sleeping I'll not wake him with such news! It can wait a little longer."

"And when you've told him? You're really leaving?"

"Another day or two of this thaw and the passes should be open," he said, looking past her toward the rugged crests of the peaks. "Perhaps, with me out of the way, there's a chance of the council reconsidering their decision. Canby and Barnhouse at least are fair-minded men, though they're outnumbered on the council. And I'm not forgetting all the things I've seen and heard these past few days.

"This valley is primed for real trouble—and if it breaks, they're going to need something a lot stronger to lean on than Bert Dakins! Maybe they'll be able to see that, once I'm gone, and think again about getting rid of Sam. . . ."

"Once you're gone—" she repeated, and pain shadowed her eyes. "What then? Will I ever hear from you again, Jim?"

He took his time answering that, for it was a problem that bothered him badly and could not be easily solved. "I just don't know," he admitted finally. "For your own good, Stella, after I'm out of your sight you should try to forget all about me. But, by God, I purely don't want that!"

"Did you think I want it?" she countered. "Oh, please! Jim, you must promise—"

"No!" he exclaimed fiercely, shaking hs head. "I'm sorry. But wherever I go from here I have to travel light. I can't carry around a load of promises. If it seems wise, and I'm able, then perhaps I'll try to get word to you. But I must always be free to do whatever I think is right!"

She bit at her lower lip as she studied his sober expression. In a small voice, then, she said, "But I will be seeing you at least once more before you leave?"

"Of course."

Silently she nodded. And he carried his problems with him as he went down the rickety steps from the ledge where the marshal's shack perched, leaving Stella looking after him—a forlorn figure, a shawl drawn about her shoulders.

Making his way back up the twisting street, he had to duck the drip from wooden awnings and pick a way through

81

the slop of thawing mud and melting snow. The dry gully that faced the long street and its single line of buildings was now filled nearly to the banks by a chocolate-colored torrent that tossed debris along its churning surface.

Even the bright sunshine, and the hopeful promise of what might be the final relaxing of winter's hard grip, could not make this town beautiful. Yet Jim Bannister regretted leaving, for he could only guess at what lay waiting for him out there beyond the pass, across the ranges. He'd have had to go soon, in any event. Still, it was hard to bear the guilty thought he was himself at least partly to blame for the situation he was leaving behind. It was poor payment to Sam White after the old lawman's kindness.

And, Stella. . .

As he came opposite the jail, the plank door opened. Bert Dakins hawked and spat into the street and then, catching sight of Bannister, stood framed there as he watched the other man go by. Sunlight made a smear of the nickeled badge pinned to his shirtfront; Bannister had already endured the man's smug triumph when he went to the jail a little earlier to collect his few personal belongings.

Aside from the discomfort of a cold in his head, Dakins was on top of the world. In one stroke he had been rid not only of the tall stranger he disliked, but of the old man who had first given him his menial job of jailkeeper. Today he stood as the symbol of the law in Morgantown, which was as high as ambition could ever take him.

But it was Stella Harbord who continued uppermost in Bannister's thoughts as he turned in at the hotel and, crossing the lobby, went down the long central corridor to his own door. He had seldom troubled to lock it and felt no particular surprise now as the knob turned and the panel swung open under his hand. But he halted, shocked into cold amazement, when he saw the woman seated in the rocker by the window, waiting for him.

Irene Youngdahl had made herself at home. Her coat and fur-trimmed hat lay on the bed. Hands folded demurely, she gazed at Bannister as though it were the most natural thing in the world for him to expect to find her here.

For his part, he was at a loss for a moment whether to

close the door or leave it wide open. Then, scowling, he kicked it shut and demanded harshly, "What is this supposed to mean?"

She smiled faintly. "That should be obvious. I wanted to see you. You were coming up the street, so I thought I'd wait."

"In my room?" he exclaimed.

"Oh, really!" With careless grace she got to her feet. "We're not children," she said, as she walked toward him. "It never occurred to me that *you* would be a prude."

"Prudery has nothing to do with it. I should think you'd have some concern over the risk of being seen."

"No risk at all," she assured him pleasantly. "There's a side entrance to this building, if you hadn't noticed. Anyone can come and go as they feel like. It's a wonder anybody ever pays his bill."

Impatient anger ground Bannister's jaw and tightened his big fists at his sides. "That's something the management can worry about!" he grunted. "Meanwhile, the sooner *you* get out of here——"

"But, I'm not," she said calmly.

She stood directly before him now, her blond head tilted back as she studied his face with a look that combined subtle mockery and a disturbing intentness. Disturbing, too, was the subtle fragrance that clung to her, and the artful way in which waist and skirt set off the lines of her figure.

"If I risked my good name in coming here, as you insist, then I assure you I certainly don't mean to go until I've finished my business."

He drew a breath. "All right," he said gruffly. "If you think you've got business with me, then let's have it over with."

"That's better." Her smile widened, but her eyes remained cool and untouched. "I understand you lost your job, Mister Bryan, though I doubt it came as any surprise."

Bannister patiently waited for her to say what was in her mind.

"You killed a man," she went on, "and lost your job. And I see you've now taken to wearing a gun. I must say it looks very natural, somehow." She let her glance slide down his solid length, to touch upon the holstered weapon a moment before lifting her eyes again to his face.

"It wasn't the first time you'd killed, was it? Or, probably, the last? From what I heard about last night, it sounds as though gunplay must come very easily for you."

"Does it?" His voice was crisp.

She seemed to study him for a long minute. And though he was half prepared for them, her next words touched him like ice: "I might have an interesting proposition for the man who'd be willing to kill someone for *me*. . . ."

Bannister stared at her, his breath shallow in his throat. She said softly, "Would you like a guess as to who that someone is?"

He swallowed. "Your husband?" he said, and he saw her red lips curve with satisfaction.

"I see I *can* talk to you," said Irene Youngdahl. "We've never really seemed to hit it off—until now, yet somehow I thought all along that you could be the one!"

"A murderer? That's hardly flattering!" he said coldly, trying to keep the revulsion from his voice.

Instantly she sobered. "But I'm only being honest! I'm paying you the compliment of thinking there's no use in varnishing facts." She came a step nearer, and now her eyes, raised to his, were intent and probing.

"Whatever else you are, you're a poor man, Mister Bryan—if that's your real name. You have a horse, and a saddle, and the clothes you stand in. And a gun that you know how to use!"

"It's no unusual combination. Why single me out? In almost any saloon you'll find a man who'll take pay to do a killing."

"Yes," she agreed, scornfully. "And hound me the rest of my life, for blackmail! Oh, no! That's not what I want!" Deliberately, then, her eyes and her voice changed and softened. She was very close and when she placed her hand on his own its touch, like the caress of her voice, held subtle seductiveness. "Not just any hired gun, Mister Bryan—a partner! One who wants the same things that I do, all the way! I'll be a rich woman, Mister Bryan, and what I have I'm willing to share—without reservation."

"It would look to me," he said, not responding, "that you stand to be richer if you keep the setup you've already got. Claude Youngdahl is an ambitious man, though he's a long way yet from his goals."

"But I loath him!" she exclaimed. Her fingers tightened on Bannister's. "I wonder if you can ever understand how it sets my teeth on edge for him to even touch me! I cannot stand it—not any longer!"

Jim Bannister looked at her for another moment. Then, quite deliberately he stepped away from her and his words were brittle with dislike. "I'm afraid you may have to stand it awhile, at any rate. You and I have no basis for doing business."

Her stare widened; she seemed unable to believe him. "You're turning me down?"

"As plainly as I know how, Mrs. Youngdahl. You'll have to do your looking in some other man's bedroom."

At that, color drained from her face. Her eyes seemed to grow until they filled it; her lips peeled back, bloodlessly, from her white teeth and then, with a hiss of rage, she brought her arm around with her palm aimed for his cheek.

Bannister had read the move in advance and his own hand came up in time to catch her wrist and check the blow. "Enough of this!" he said gruffly. Raging, she fought to pull free, then fell against him and it was a moment before he realized she was trying to reach the gun in his holster.

He felt it start to slide from the leather. With a grunt of anger and surprise he shoved her away and she stumbled backward, against the brass bedstead. There she caught herself and stood empty-handed, glaring her fury.

The sleek blond hairdo had come partly undone from its pins; for the first time her controls were gone and she showed him, in her glaring eyes and swelling breasts, the image of a woman infuriated beyond reason.

Quickly enough, however, she got herself in hand again. Her breathing settled; her voice was a taut whiplash as she called him a name he had never heard before on a woman's lips.

"Now you're wasting your breath!" Jim Bannister chided her.

Irene Youngdahl whirled, snatched up her coat and fur-trimmed hat from the bed and stormed past him to the door. But with her hand on the knob she paused to hurl a tremulous, whispered warning: "If you ever breathe a word of this to anyone, I'll—I'll—"

Bannister's lip curled tightly. With cutting irony he said, "Do I look the type to betray a lady's secrets?"

There was nothing beautiful about her as she absorbed that, hating him with her eyes, contained by her own unbearable fury. Then, with no apparent caution against being discovered leaving his room, she simply wrenched the door open and stormed out, leaving it standing wide. Jim Bannister closed it after her.

She had left a trace of the subtle scent she wore. To his nostrils it seemed, just then, very offensive indeed.

Out on the street a ranch wagon bucked its way through the thawing black mud that let it drop nearly to the axles and had the driver cursing his team as they slipped and pawed for footing.

A couple of ranchers, fined down by the long winter, stood on the sidewalk and squinted at the dazzling sunlight and speculated as to whether this would actually last and herald a new season and the opening of the passes to the outside world.

It was just as likely, in this treacherous country, that another change could come to freeze everything tighter than the hubs of hell as it also froze a man's hopes within his breast.

Irene Youngdahl, leaving the hotel, was still in a savage mood after the humiliating experience of being spurned by someone she considered no better than a killer and an adventurer; but she had managed to regain some composure and to put her appearance in order, trapping the loose strands of hair and pushing them back under the edges of the fur cap. When she heard someone call to her she stopped and turned, presenting a controlled and icy surface as she saw Stella Harbord hurrying toward her.

It was the first time there had been any exchange between them, and Irene looked at the Harbord woman with unyielding dislike. There could hardly have been a greater contrast between the well-groomed banker's wife, and the other in her shabby cloth coat. Nothing she could have to say promised to hold any interest, and Irene answered curtly, "I'm afraid I have no time just now."

Stella Harbord's strong, work-roughened hands twisted together in her anxiety. "It's terribly important. And I'm sure you could help—if you only would."

"Help?" Curiosity held Irene now, standing there in the thin sunlight amid the bustle of the reviving town. "Very well," she said impatiently. "What is it?"

"It concerns poor Sam White. I'm Stella Harbord. . . ."

"Yes, I know who you are."

"I've been acting as Sam's nurse and housekeeper during this time while he's laid up. And—well, perhaps you know he lost his job last night?"

"I suppose I heard something about that," the blond woman said indifferently. "In fact I heard there was a killing of some sort, and that the mayor made a clean sweep of the marshal's office."

Stella Harbord nodded. "That's true. Jim Bryan was fired at the same time. But Jim's a young man, and so with him it isn't that important. . . ."

Irene looked sharply at the other woman, through suddenly narrowed eyes. So it's *Jim,* she thought, and a spear of jealousy stabbed her. It began to appear there might have been more going on here than she had understood; perhaps it explained why her own plans for the tall stranger seemed to have gone awry. If, that is, Jim Bryan could actually prefer, instead of her, someone like this plain, work-gaunted gambler's wench!

All this time Stella Harbord was continuing, spilling out her plea in a tumble of anxious speech: "—and since, after all, it wasn't really any of Sam White's doing that Reub Hodem was killed, it seems hardly fair—after all the years he's served this town—"

"Just a minute!" Irene broke in with angry impatience. "What are you talking about, anyway? What in the world do you expect *me* to do?"

Taken aback, the other woman stammered a little. "Why, after all, your husband is an important member of the

87

council. Anything he has to say would carry tremendous weight. I was hoping perhaps you'd speak to him—help him see this thing from Sam White's point of view. Because, to fire him like this, without the least word of warning—"

Irene interrupted crisply: "Come now! It was hardly without warning. The old man must have known long before last night that the council had decided to let him go. I know for a fact that Bryan knew it."

"Yes, but he never told Sam. Sam's had enough to bear without that to worry him. Even now, he hasn't learned what happened last night. That's why I'm trying to do what I can, before he does learn. Just on the chance it might do some good, I mean to talk to Mister Canby and Doctor Barnhouse about trying to change the council's decision. And, even a single word to your husband—"

"I have not the slightest intension of interfering with the business of the city council," Irene Youngdahl said flatly, deciding to put an end to this. "I can't be bothered about any worn-out has-been of a peace officer." She added, with a certain slashing, malicious pleasure, "Certainly not to please some tinhorn gambler's wife—assuming you actually *were* his wife, which I doubt!"

She might as well have slapped the woman. Stella Harbord's head and shoulders jerked and her face lost color. A broken cry of protest came from her, but by then Irene Youngdahl had turned and left her, nursing an inward satisfaction that did not show on her impassive exterior.

Yet it was still not enough. She had given vent to some of her stunned fury against Jim Bryan; but there was a residue, like a burning acid, that rose again to gall her pride and make her seethe. Now as she moved quickly along the boardwalk, more than one townsman lifted his hat politely to the banker's wife, but she failed to notice. Something the Harbord woman had let slip was working in her head, giving her the clue she needed and exploding suddenly into full-blown decision.

She was sometimes a creature of impulse, and with an idea like this in possession of her there was no other thing but to let it have its way. Minutes later she had reached Sam

88

White's shanty and deliberately climbed the crooked flight of steps to the door.

She knocked a second time before a querulous voice, somewhere within, called out gruffly, "The door's open." She shrugged her shoulders, lifted the latch, and stepped inside.

As a normal thing she would not willingly have entered such a place. She looked about her with disdain for its air of poverty, of hand-me-down respectability. From beyond the half-open bedroom door Sam White's voice spoke again: "Who's there?"

"It's Mrs. Youngdahl," she answered, and walked in. She could barely repress her laughter as she saw the astonishment on the face of the man in bed.

Sam White, propped against the pillows, with his thinning mop of hair awry, clutched the blankets tight against his chin. She cut off his stammered question. "If I embarrass you, I'll go away. But I was passing by and thought I really should stop in."

The old bachelor found his tongue. "Why—why, sure. Yes, ma'am! I thank you!" He looked a little wildly about the dingy room. "I ain't exactly set up for visitors. That chair, yonder—"

"I won't sit," she answered quickly without moving from the doorway. "This can only be a moment."

"Yes, ma'am," the old lawman said again.

"Please understand," she said, "I'm not criticizing my husband; I know that he and the council do what they have to do. But this time, I can't help disagreeing with them."

Utter bafflement and the beginning of troubled concern worked their way into the man's weathered face. "I don't reckon I quite follow you . . ."

She pretended to misunderstand. "Now you're only being modest. No one could possibly deny that you did your job well—at least, while you were able. Certainly you deserve something better from Morgantown than to be dismissed without even a chance to—" It was then she appeared to recognize the utter bewilderment in the old man's face. She let her eyes go wide as she exclaimed, "But—you don't *know*!"

He swallowed, in a throat that seemed to have gone dry. He said hoarsely, "I'd appreciate if you'd speak plain, Mrs. Youngdahl. Just what are you telling me?"

"It shouldn't be left for me to tell you!" she declared indignantly. "Where *is* this Jim Bryan? Hasn't he the nerve to admit he brought this all to a head last night—by committing murder while wearing the marshal's badge?"

"I don't believe that!" Sam White retorted sharply, then his certainty appeared to weaken a little. "Who's he supposed to have murdered?"

"The blacksmith. A man named Hodem."

"Reub Hodem?"

"I believe that was his first name. All I know is that Mayor Ries took Bryan's badge away from him, then and there, and said he was cleaning out the marshal's office. And now that little man, Dakins, is wearing the badge until the council brings in someone permanent. Mister White," she added, seriously, "just how much do you really know about that Bryan fellow? It's true you had him appointed as your deputy, but I wonder if you knew he's been meeting with the council—secretly?"

His thunderous look answered her. She went on: "I saw them, myself—just the other day, in our parlor. I heard some discussion of his taking your job over, and I thought it was strange behavior for someone who was supposed to be indebted to you. Well, I suppose now it's neither here nor there." She raised her coat collar, preparing to take her leave.

"I'm terribly afraid I've upset you, Mister White—and here I only came on a friendly impulse to say how sorry I am about what's happened. I'm sure, though, you'll find another job somewhere. . . ."

She smiled pleasantly, but behind the smile her eyes coolly measured the effect her words had had. What she saw in Sam White's face was enough to cause a small, spiteful satisfaction make itself felt through the savage resentment left from that scene in the hotel room.

As she walked out of the house, into the sunlight, she would have known an even keener satisfaction had she seen what happened next.

Sam White lay like one stricken, staring sightlessly at the cracked plaster of the ceiling. Suddenly one hand, lying atop the blankets, began to twitch and tremble and his mouth pulled into a grimace.

"Would he do that to me?" he cried aloud, into the stillness. "After—after—"

His hands gripped the blanket, flung it savagely from him; he rolled over and came to a sit on the edge of the bed. At the sudden unaccustomed movement after so many months a wave of weakness went through his frame and he clung to the bedstead a moment, squatting there in a pair of longjohns, with head hanging and bare feet braced upon the cold floorboards.

The healed-over bullet wound in his leg throbbed wildly for a moment; but that eased, and presently he found the strength to push himself to his feet. Using the wooden frame of the bed as a prop he looked about the room, waiting out a brief spasm of dizziness that made it rock and sway around him.

Stella, he had learned, was a most meticulous house-keeper. His suit would be hanging in the closet, the rest of his clothing folded neatly away in a drawer of the warped-top pine dresser. And his gun?

He took a tentative step, then another. The room swayed and settled; he was, he realized with a swelling sense of relief, stronger than he would have expected. Perhaps he really was completely well, as that fool Henry Barnhouse had been insisting for so long now. Well enough, at last, he promised himself, to do what he had to do.

Jim Bannister! That traitor!

He gained the dresser, leaned a palm on top of it while his other hand fumbled at the knob and pulled the drawer open. Yes, there were his shirts and his extra suit of underwear, socks and handkerchiefs. And, nestled among them, his gun in its holster with the scuffed leather shell belt, cartridge-studded, wrapped about them.

Sam White grunted in satisfaction, and reached to lift out the weapon.

91

CHAPTER X

Jim Bannister, depressed and at loose ends from his encounter with Irene Youngdahl, shut the door with revulsion on his neat hotel room where the scene had taken place.

Outside on the street he paused to build a cigarette and light it, and stood a moment contemplating the high walls of the gulch, scarred by old mine workings and capped by the clean blue sky ceiling. He wondered again as to the condition of the passes. He had heard speculation that a freight rig with a stout team might be able to buck them very shortly, if this weather change continued.

Well, the sooner he was able to quit this place the better for everyone, but he still faced a difficult task that could be put off no longer. Perhaps, by now, Sam White was awake. There was no sense in postponing any longer the agony of confronting him.

Deliberately he flung aside the unfinished smoke, and turned in the direction of White's shanty. He had covered less than a block of the distance when he saw a man who stepped away from the brick front of a building where he had been leaning in the sunshine, tentatively raising a hand.

It was the homestead rancher, Ira Steigel—the lath-lean, pale-eyed man whose shabby figure always seemed to exude a sour odor of defeat and beaten spirit. There was a look of half-formed resolve about the weak arrangement of his features, just now, as though some decision he had taken might quickly melt and evaporate. He announced, in a halting stammer, "Mister Bryan, I been looking for you. There's something I just got to see you about."

Bannister frowned. "All right."

"Not here! Not right out in the open!" The pale eyes scooted past Bannister and anxiously searched the street. He turned back to clutch at Bannister's arm. "I just don't know what might happen if it ever got out I come to you!"

His anxiety intrigued Bannister. "Back here," he said, and pulled Stiegel with him into the passageway between adjoining buildings. There were no windows here, and a shallow doorway opened a recess where they could talk without being seen from the street. He pushed the man into this, checked again to satisfy himself that no one was watching. "Well? What's your problem?"

The man seemed to be wavering, almost ready to back down from what he had started. He said anxiously, "You won't tell? You won't let it out where you heard?"

"No, of course not," he promised impatiently.

"I figured I could depend on it. . . ." Ira Stiegel filled his lungs, a shuddering breath. "It's Gil Rickman," he blurted. "And some of them others. They're about to make a play."

Bannister's eyes narrowed, as a whole, complex problem he had nearly lost sight of came thrusting itself again to his attention. "You mean—against Tate Pauling?"

The other nodded. "I guess you've knowed it was coming all right—after the way that black Irishman, Sullivan, combed us out the other evening when we found Tate drunk in the alley. Sullivan knew what he was talking about, Bryan. There's been a lot of hard feelings. And now that the booze has put the skids under Pauling, there's some of us have been getting together to try and figure out ways to give him a push."

"That's what that crowd was up to Sunday, at Rickman's?"

"Sure. Gil was scared to death when you showed up, that afternoon—afraid you'd catch wind of what was going on. He nearly wet his britches waiting till you left. Actually there wasn't any decision taken at the meeting; but last night we had us another one—and that time there was."

And in between those two meetings, Jim Bannister thought with disturbing clarity, Gil Rickman—or someone who smoked the same repulsive brand of pipe tobacco—had climbed the hill to make a call on Claude Youngdahl, and left by the back way. . . . He filed that away for what it was worth. "And what was decided? What's the play?"

Ira Stiegel swallowed hard. There were beads of sweat along the hair line at his temple as he pulled scabbed fingers through his straggle of gray-shot whiskers. "Oh, God!" he exclaimed, a little wildly. "If I say, they're *bound* to know it was me that—"

Exasperated, Bannister took the man by a shoulder of his threadbare jacket. "Now that you've started," he said grimly, "you better make up your mind to finish this!"

The other met his cold look, and he nodded in resignation. "Sure, Bryan. . . . The play is, they're going after Tepee's stack yard. What's left of his winter feed, that Pauling cut and put by to get him through till spring thaw, is all there in one place. So they're gonna fire it."

Bannister let his hand drop. His eyes were cold, his mind busy with a dozen chasing thoughts as he stared hard at the other man. He said, at last, "Risky, isn't it? You'll start a war! You're all vulnerable; you've all got feed that can be burnt. If I was Grady Sullivan I'm damned if I wouldn't give it back to every one of you in the same coin. And with the Tepee crew behind him, Grady's enough of a scrapper to do just that!"

Stiegel nodded dumbly. "I know. I tried to tell 'em. But who ever listened to me?" He lifted bony shoulders. "Not Gil Rickman! He won't have it any other way. And he's sure got one hell of a loud voice. When he starts using it—that crowd listens!"

"So, it's all Rickman!" Bannister murmured, half to himself, gazing at the alley mud.

"Yes sir. . . . I've had me one hell of a night, trying to figure what I should do. I feel like a traitor, turning against my kind, but—well, I'm afraid there's a little more yet, than what I've told you!"

Bannister looked at him sharply. "Yes?"

"I hung around after the meeting, trying to get a word with Rickman; I overheard him and Dave Pitts talking. I couldn't hardly believe my ears, but I swear Gil was saying, in so many words, that burning the stacks was only to be bait for a trap. They didn't figure to tell the others; but the idea is that the fire will bring Sullivan and the Tepee crew, there'll be shooting, and during it somebody's to cut Sullivan down in cold blood!"

"You sure of this?" Bannister's face was iron.

Ira Stiegel nodded emphatically. "They mean to *murder* him, Mister Bryan! They figure, with him out of the way, there'll be nobody left to fight Tate Pauling's war for him. Then Tepee will fall to pieces, just for the pickin' up. And I reckon they could be right. . . ."

Considering Tate Pauling's state of deterioration, it very possibly was. Bannister conceded the point, as he stood there in the litter of the alleyway and absorbed the stunning news this scarecrow of a man had given him.

He did not doubt for a moment that Stiegel was telling the truth of what he had overheard. Lying about such a matter was beyond his courage and his capacity for guile.

Scowling, Bannister asked, "What have you done about this? Who have you told?"

"I never did nothing, and I never told anybody at all—not till this minute! If it should get back to Rickman—my God, he'd *kill* me!" The man pawed at Bannister's arm with shaking fingers. "That's why you got to keep me out of it, whatever you do. You promised!"

Well, and what *did* he mean to do? Except as it was important to Sam White, anything the ranchers of Morgan Valley did to one another had never been any affair of his; and now it should mean even less, were it not for one fact: Even though Grady Sullivan was no responsibility of his, and in spite of Grady's blind loyalty to a man like Pauling, Bannister liked the stubborn little Irishman. Not to act now, at least to the extent of passing on Ira Stiegel's warning, would make him partly responsible if the Tepee foreman should ride into a trap and maybe even to his death.

This was the thought that held him frowning and impatient but definitely bothered. He rubbed a palm across his cheeks and said, "When's this party scheduled to come off?"

"I'm not certain. They'll be gathering at Gil Rickman's in another hour or so—but not me! I decided I'm gonna get myself lost. Come down with a bellyache or something, so the missus has to put me to bed. I want no part of this!"

"All right," Bannister said heavily. "Thanks for the tip.

You go about your business. I'll try to see you're not involved." He gave Ira Stiegel plenty of time to make his escape down the alleyway.

Several minutes after the rancher had ambled away at his peculiar, loose-coupled gait, Bannister again emerged upon the main street sidewalk, reasonably sure no one had witnessed the meeting.

By this time his mind was made up. As little taste as he had for pulling Tate Pauling's chestnuts out of the fire he had to get a warning to Sullivan at once. It was not a message he could entrust to anyone. He would have to carry it himself.

His bay horse had never been removed from the stall in the jail shed, where he had been in the custom of keeping it and where his saddle and gear were stored now. The shed stood backed against a low spur, at the edge of the second growth pine timber where Bannister had occasionally chopped firewood for the jail. It was a crude, low building with a slanting tarpaper roof, containing stalls enough for a half dozen horses but seldom holding that many. Just now it contained, besides the bay, only Sam White's blue roan.

Bannister had grained and watered both animals himself that morning, not trusting Bert Dakins with the job, and so he knew the bay was fed and in good shape for a ride. In the dim light of the shed he backed the horse out into the aisle, put on the bridle and spread the blanket over its back. He took his saddle off the stall partition where it was racked and swung it into place, got it cinched down.

He was tightening the latigo in the cinch ring when a faint stir of sound behind him—like a careful footstep muffled in loose straw—suddenly caught his ear.

Preoccupation with his own business, and the covering sounds he himself was making, had for the moment stilled his ingrained instincts for caution. Now, half bent as he was, he whirled with surprising swiftness for one so big.

Slick straw slipped beneath his boots. He glimpsed the shape of a man looming over him—no, there were two of them. His palm struck the butt of his revolver, swept it from the holster.

96

Then the clubbing weight of a gun's barrel chopped down, hard. Even though cushioned by the felt of his Stetson, it was a blow to crush a man to insensibility. Bannister's head seemed to explode in a dazzling burst of light that gave instant place to engulfing darkness.

Virg Clausen, standing over the man he had felled, grinned and slid his gun back into the holster. "So far we get the breaks!" he grunted. "We don't even have to saddle his horse—he went and done it for us. . . ."

His partner, back from taking a hurried look through the door at the nearby jail, said nervously, "I don't think anybody heard anything, but we better hurry and get him out of here!"

"There's no rush. Dakins ain't at the jail—we just saw him leave." But the redhead was scarcely less anxious than Billy Ide himself. Though the unconscious man was plainly due to remain that way for some time, as a precaution Clausen gagged him with his own handkerchief and secured his wrists and ankles with lengths of rope they found on a peg.

Together they hefted their victim's limp weight up and across the saddle of his horse, belly down. Virg Clausen picked up the big man's Stetson and hung it on the saddlehorn. By the time this was done, the increasing danger of discovery had them working fast and Billy Ide was querulous as he begged the other to hurry with the knots. Clausen cursed him to silence.

After another check from the shed door, the redhead announced, "The coast is still clear. There's a gully just behind this shed. Take him up into the trees and wait there for me while I go clean out his hotel room."

"What about my bronc?"

"I'll bring it to you, along with his stuff."

"Just don't waste any time!" Billy Ide said sourly. "Damn it, I don't want to get caught with this guy on my hands!"

"What have you got to worry about?" the redhead grunted. "I'm the one's got the tricky end of the business!"

He took a final look, then motioned Billy Ide out of the shed, leading the bay with its limp burden swaying on its back.

The horse didn't like any part of this, and balked; the blond man cursed and hauled at the reins, and Clausen gave it a slap on the rump to start it moving. He watched as, with almost frantic haste, Billy Ide went off at a sprint leading the bay along the side of the shed, toward the shelter of the gully and the trees; afterward, when his partner was gone from sight, Clausen drew a freer breath.

At the last moment he remembered and, going back into the shed, hunted around in the straw until he found the gun that had fallen out of the tall stranger's holster; he drew a shallow breath, realizing what a bad mistake it would have been to leave it there for someone else to find. He shoved it behind his belt, under his coat. After a final look around to make certain he'd missed nothing else, he left.

At the front corner of the jail he paused a moment to survey the street. When he saw no indication that his movements were being observed, it occurred to him this could be the best time—with Bert Dakins gone—to complete the business he had waiting in the jail office.

A glance through the barred window showed him no one inside. The door was unlocked. Boldly, because that was the way he tackled any matter, Virg Clausen walked in, heeled the door shut, and looked quickly around the empty office.

He understood that what he wanted would be in the battered desk; he went to it, quickly, and tried the drawers. And in the second one he opened, in a cardboard box without a lid, he found what he was looking for. A grunt of satisfaction broke from Clausen's lips.

Suddenly he froze, his head jerking as a shadow fell upon the barred front window. It was Dakins, and with a quick movement Clausen pulled his gun. But the door did not open, and a moment later he once more saw the new marshal's silhouette cross the window.

Carrying the gun, Virg Clausen moved lightly around the desk and to a second window, from where he could see Dakins making his way toward the horse shed at the back of the lot. Eyes narrowing, he wondered if Dakins had noticed something wrong back there, but decided that was not likely.

Meanwhile, he had been granted a moment and he must make the best of it. Again at the desk, he scooped what he had found into a pocket of his blanket coat and kneed the drawer shut. He went to the door, cracked it open; then, with the gun once more in its holster, he stepped unhurriedly through.

Squinting against the stab of sunlight reflected from dripping icicles and puddles of melted water in the street, he took a quick look around before starting away in the direction of the hotel. It was then that he caught sight of a man making his painful way along the warped sidewalk, apparently leaning his weight heavily on the handle of a cane. He would almost have thought it looked like the former marshal, Sam White, except that he knew White was in bed and had been for months. It did not matter. Clausen dismissed the puzzle with an incurious shrug, and turned his back.

What had been planned with such care was going according to schedule, and no hitch yet. But with Billy Ide and the unconscious prisoner waiting on him, he had better not lose any time.

Sam White was learning the hard way that a man did not spend four months on his back without showing the effects. Not only the tissues of that hurt leg—mended but until now untested—but his whole body betrayed a shaky weakness that made him feel his age, and was a cruel reminder that perhaps his enemies were right and he was no longer fit for office.

Vaguely, he was beginning to suspect it might have been just such fears that had kept him down so long, even after Henry Barnhouse insisted he was well enough to be up and about again. Maybe he had half-consciously dreaded learning the worst. And—a vicious circle—every day he refused to try himself had only helped drain his confidence.

But with the aid of his cane, and with anger to spur him, Sam was managing well enough. He limped into the jail office, hot words ready to tumble from his lips, and then

99

stood a moment uncertain and frustrated by the realization no one was there. He was turning to leave when Bert Dakins came edging through the door, snuffling from the cold in his head, and with an armload of chopped wood for the empty firebox. He stopped dead at sight of the old man. His jaw dropped. "Sam!" he blurted. "You supposed to be on your feet?"

"It's damn well time I was!" Sam White said. Dakins sidled in, kicking the door shut, and dropped his load of wood in the box by the stove. He straightened, absently brushing at his clothes and in so doing touched the marshal's badge pinned to his coat; he went motionless, glanced quickly at Sam.

The latter was staring at the badge in a way that made Dakins flush slightly and bunch his jaw muscles.

"There's been some changes," he said, too loudly. "You ain't the marshal no longer. The mayor himself give me this badge, and I'm in my rights to wear it."

The old man wagged his head. "I know," he said tiredly. "I heard what happened. I ain't holding it against you." His faded eyes sparked with an inner heat. "Right now I'm looking for Ban—for Jim Bryan. Where is he?"

"Gosh, Sam, I don't know. He don't work here no more, either. He was in awhile ago, to pick up some personal truck, and I told him he'd better be taking his animal out of the shed—I told him the city wasn't gonna pay for keeping it any longer. I checked out there just now and the bay is gone; so, I guess he's been and got it."

"Thanks." The old man sighed. He gave a hitch to the belted gun that seemed too heavy a weight to strap around his wasted frame, and swung toward the door. There, he turned back to tell the man who had been his jailer: "If you can put up with my stuff for a little longer, I'll try to get it out of your way as soon as I can. Or you could just dump it into a box or something, and I'll have somebody pick it up. . . ."

Bert Dakins looked suddenly embarrassed. "Hell, Sam! There's no hurry. And that blue roan in the shed—reckon it won't hurt nobody if you was to leave it where it is for a while."

"Don't let Morgantown do me any favors," the old lawman grunted. "I'll find some other place to keep him." He jerked the door open.

Curiosity got the better of Dakins. "You have business with that Bryan fellow, Sam? Should I tell him you're looking for him?"

Sam White showed him a face like iron. "Yeah. I'm looking for him. . . ."

In a village the size of Morgantown, there were few enough places to look. Making his way up the gulch street, Sam White was met everywhere by pleased surprise, tempered by signs of embarrassment over what the town had done to him. Sam was impatient of both. He had one thing in mind, and in his determination to get on with it he cut short any attempt to make conversation.

Even so, he could not fail to note the quickening pulse of life around him. The business houses that had remained open through the long winter had their shelves nearly empty now, as the last of their stock of goods neared depletion. Unless the opening of the passes came soon, with the arrival of the first supply wagons from outside, Morgantown would really feel the pinch.

There had been prolonged winters when men on webs had had to beat their way out and bring back supplies enough on their own shoulders to keep Morgantown going through the last bitter weeks of freeze. But today there was a spirit of optimism, a feeling that the break was very near.

At Irwin's barber shop, someone was even making up a pool and taking bets as to the hour, and day, of the first arrival in town of a rig and team from beyond the ranges. It was said that riders had already left to bring back a report on the condition of the pass road.

It was in the group at Irwin's that Sam found Lloyd Canby. The storekeeper was in the chair, but he whipped the towel off and hurried into the street when Sam merely shoved his head in for a look and backed out again. Impatiently, the old man had to listen to Canby's stammered questions, his concern over Sam's state of health.

"I'm all right," he insisted gruffly, rapping the end of his walking stick against the muddy, sodden boards underfoot.

"Barnhouse has been telling me a long time that I was. It just took a shock to get me on my feet."

Bareheaded in the sunshine, Canby colored slightly under the lather drying on his face. "I know what you must be thinking, Sam," he exclaimed. "Stella Harbord was combing me out on this same subject not more than ten minutes ago. But you ought to know neither me nor Henry was in favor of letting you go. We fought it in the council as long as we could. Still, this Bryan fellow was your man; and after what he did last night, we wasn't left with much room to argue. Honest to God, though—"

Sam cut him off, with a lifted hand and an impatient swing of his head. He said bluntly, "All that is ancient history. I'm gonna ask you one question and I want a yes or a no answer: Was there really talk between him and the council—at any time—about him taking my job, for good?"

The storekeeper blinked. "Why, yes," he admitted. "There was. As a matter of fact—"

"That's all I want to know," Sam White said shortly. And he left his friend staring after him and went stomping off up the street, the end of his cane thumping angrily.

Using the leg seemed actually to be taking some of the stiffness out of it, but he had overworked himself in climbing this steep street too quickly. There was a shakiness in his limbs and his heart was pounding. When he came abreast of the livery stable he would have gone past it except that the hostler came out the big door just then. Sam asked his question: "Did that fellow Bryan leave a bay horse here, the past half hour or so?"

Leaning on his pitchfork the man shook his head. "Bryan? Ain't seen anything of the murdering bastard. . ."

Sam thanked him with a nod, but his glance was withdrawn and abstracted; already a dark suspicion was taking form. A few doors beyond stood the big hotel building. Suddenly he was sure he would find the answer to his search there.

By the time he had climbed the five steps to the verandah his knees were shaking and he had to lean against a roof support and rest for a moment. Tom Lawton, the balding, sourfaced owner, was behind the lobby desk and he gave a

102

startled exclamation when Sam entered; the latter cut him off. "Which room is Bryan's?"

"Number six. Back down the hall. You like me to see if he's in?" Lawton started to lift the drop gate of the desk. "You don't look like you should be on your feet, Sam!"

The old man waved him off. "I'll look for myself," he said, and moved resolutely across the lobby with its faded carpet and high ceiling and wallpaper stained by time. He found number six and, leaning heavily on his cane, knocked with a hand that trembled slightly. There was no answer, no sound of movement inside. Grasping the knob, he felt the unlocked door give. He pushed it open.

He looked at the evidence of a hasty departure. The closet door stood wide, on emptiness. Bureau drawers had been yanked open and left that way, rifled of their contents. Every scrap of personal belongings had been removed by someone in a hurry who evidently had no intention of coming back.

Sam White closed his eyes for a moment. Soundlessly, bitterly, his lips formed a single searing curse. Afterward, pulling his shoulders straight, he heeled around and made his slow and torturous way again into the lobby. He looked at Tom Lawton and told the hotelman roughly, "Appears to me you've lost a roomer. Bryan's gone, and everything with him."

"What! And him owing me two weeks' rent?" Lawton's face turned angry red and he slammed back the drop gate. "My God, let me see, once!"

Within moments he was back, shaking with anger. "Damn if he hasn't pulled out! Where to, I wonder?"

"He could be on his way across the pass by now," Sam White said heavily. "He's taken his horse—I already checked."

"Shows you never can tell about anyone! He always kept his bill paid, before. I can see that he might be mad at the town, but I wouldn't of thought he'd take it out on *me*! I never made him any trouble. I figured, since he was a friend of yours—"

"He's no friend of mine!" old Sam muttered savagely.

Lawton looked at him sharply. The old lawman was

leaning heavily against the desk, his face the color of old ashes. The other man exclaimed, "Sam! You look awful!" He took Sam White by one arm. "You better come in here. . ."

There was a sagging but comfortable-looking leather couch in the hotel's office. Lawton led him in there, and without protest Sam let himself be placed on the couch. From his desk the landlord took a bottle and glass and poured a stiff shot, which Sam accepted with trembling fingers and managed to get down, though it brought tears to his eyes. Tom Lawton took the glass away from him then and pressed him firmly back, got a pillow under his head and his feet lifted.

"Now, you take it easy! You can't climb onto your feet, after four months in bed, and make out like nothing had ever happened to you." He added, "I think I better get word to Doc . . . or Miz Harbord."

Sam White moved his head on the pillow. "No—no," he insisted. "I'll be all right. Don't bother anybody. Just let me rest a few minutes." He closed his eyes.

"You go right ahead. I'll see you ain't bothered." Lawton took a moment to check the draft in the wood burner; looked again at the drawn face on the pillow and, shaking his head, went out carefully pulling the door shut behind him.

Alone in the stillness of the office, Sam White spoke softly, his gray lips scarcely moving: "Damn you, Bannister! I hope you suffer for the way you've paid me back. I hope you swing!"

CHAPTER XI

In a forgotten brush-choked pocket, somewhere in the hills, Jim Bannister dug. The spade had a dull bit and the ground was a mixture of snow and frozen soil and decomposing granite, broken off the rock face that lifted beside him. He

104

worked stolidly and mechanically, making slow but definite progress.

Leaning once, to get a good hold on a boulder and heave it up out of the hole he was excavating, he felt the nausea of the ache in his skull and straightened to rest a moment with closed eyes until the throbbing eased.

He put a hand to the side of his head and winced as he touched the spot where a revolver's barrel had struck. It could have cracked the bone, but hadn't. There was a tender knot, however, and the hair above it was sticky with dried blood.

Yonder, Billy Ide gave warning: "Keep busy, there! We ain't taking all day for this little job, mister."

Bannister deliberately turned to look at him. A cold wind whistled in the rock faces and rattled the dry brush, and Billy Ide had moved out into the thin sunlight for whatever comfort it could give him; he leaned against a boulder, hunch-shouldered, one hand thrust into a coat pocket and the other weighted down by a sixgun. He raised the gun now and sunlight made a smear along its barrel, glinted on the scar that showed white against his windwhipped cheek. "Get to work!" he ordered sharply.

Bannister's mouth flattened a trifle. He stared at the other, unflinching. "I'm in no hurry to finish this hole so you can put me in it. Anyway, I don't really reckon you'll shoot —you'd just have to finish the job yourself."

"I wouldn't need to shoot you all at once," Billy Ide reminded him. "I could take off a chink here and there—fix you so you could still dig, all right, but you'd be begging me to put an end to you!" A cruel pleasure twisted the knife-scarred face, and the gun's hammer clicked back under the pull of his thumb. "I got a couple of things with you that never have been settled. You're tempting me, big fellow!"

With a shrug Bannister reached again for the long-handled spade, set its bit and shoved it deep with a thrust of his boot. He levered out a spadeful of gritty dirt, and tossed it aside onto the growing heap of loose dirt beside the hole that was meant to be his grave.

Watching him work, the blond man lapsed into a sullen, discontented scowl. His mouth worked and suddenly, into the quiet broken only by the scrape of the blade and the voice of the wind and the stomping of their horses tied nearby, he blurted out: "You don't seem very curious about what's going to happen to you!"

"Why, now, I imagine you'll tell me," Bannister said, with a touch of dry humor pulling the corners of his lips. "I just have an idea you couldn't hold back from telling it." That raised a flush on the other's angry face, darkening it and making the knife scar stand out more clearly. Jim Bannister went on working at his deliberate pace, and a moment later he was proved right. Billy Ide fairly shouted at him.

"You damned right, I mean to tell you! It wouldn't be half the fun if you didn't know just what will go on while you lie rotting in that hole!" He edged away from the boulder and came closer, into the shadow, the better to see his prisoner's expression as he told it. He said: "While I'm taking care of you, my partner is down below waiting for nightfall—with the duplicate keys out of that desk in the jail office."

Bannister went still; holding the spade he straightened slowly, and saw Billy Ide's grin widen as this news had its jarring effect.

"You hadn't thought about that, had you? Your friend Bert Dakins was the one give us the idea. And when Virg brought me the stuff from your hotel room he said he'd managed to get into the jail, all right, and helped himself to the keys he'll be wanting.

"So, everything's set. Tonight, he'll use those keys to clean out the tills in every one of the stores along the gulch; and the vault at the bank, too, if he can figure a way to crack it."

Bannister's eyes had gone narrow as he heard this. "One man—to clean out a whole town, single-handed? Sounds to me your partner has really bit off a chunk!"

"That's how he wanted it," Billy Ide said with a shrug. "Getting rid of you was my assignment . . . which suits me fine!"

"And just what does getting rid of me have to do with it?"

The blond drifter greeted the question with a bark of mocking laughter. "You ain't quite so smart, are you,

106

Bryan? I'd thought you could have figured it out by now. Who is it whose name is suddenly mud around that town, after being kicked out of his job? Who is it that's apt to be holding a grudge—and who are people going to think of when they learn that the keys that were used came out of the jail desk?"

"I guess I see it," Bannister said grimly.

"Of course you do. And you see why it has to be a one-man job. When they find out you and your horse are gone, and all your personal truck missing from your hotel room, they're gonna cuss you for a slippery skunk that used this way of getting even with Morgantown. They'll figure they've seen the last of you—and the joke is they'll never know how right they are."

"Meaning," Bannister finished for him, in a voice of iron, "that I'll be lying up here under six feet of rock and dirt, while you and your partner can ride out of Morgantown any time you feel like it with the money in your own saddle rolls. . . ." He wondered how funny the joke would be if they ever guessed that, all unsuspecting, they had left twelve thousand dollars buried in the hole he was digging. But he said: "Which of you thought up this way of paying me back? I'd hardly have credited either one of you with that kind of brains!"

What appeared to be a grudging compliment had somehow ended as an insult, and Billy Ide's pleased smirk turned suddenly ugly. "All right, you bastard! We'll see who's got the brains!" In his quick anger the gun lifted and he took a step toward Bannister, eyes blazing.

The bit of the spade, its long handle converted into a club in the tall man's grasp, made a bright, streaking arc aimed at the man with the gun. Bannister, hoping to lure him that one further yard and bring him within reach had been poised and waiting for this chance; but luck was not with him. The reach was a shade too far and he knew that even as he made his swing he would miss.

He lunged forward, trying for extra inches, but that only threw him off balance. The spade swung itself out of his grasp and went clattering as he fell forward to his knees at the edge of the hole, and heard Billy Ide's yell of startled

107

anger. Kneeling there he cringed to meet the weight of a bullet.

Instead there was the harsh sound of the man's breathing. "Oh, no you don't! Oh, no!"

Bannister raised his head and saw the eyes shining with wariness and the lips pulled back, twisted out of shape by that scar. Billy Ide's hand, holding the gun, trembled with the wish to use it. "You almost had me then!" he admitted hoarsely. "Well, that's all right—you'll get yours, only it ain't time. You ain't finished your job yet. Now, on your feet!"

Prodded by a gesture of the gunbarrel, not saying a word, Jim Bannister got up off his knees. The spade had landed some dozen feet away, out in the center of the gully. "Go get it," the man ordered. "And remember, the next phony move you try . . . well, just don't!"

Bannister drew a long breath. He didn't need to be told that he had missed his one chance. He had hoarded it, waiting for the one moment when he could use the spade— his only weapon. Instead luck had run against him, and his failure meant there was no hope of surprise. Now his enemy would be alerted, careful to stay out of his reach and quick to shoot at the first suspicious move.

Well, that was the life of a fugitive—playing the chances, accepting the fall of the cards. So far, in his months on the dodge, luck had been good to him. Someday it had to turn. He had no regrets.

He climbed up out of the grave with that gunmuzzle following his every movement, and Billy Ide sidling away to give him plenty of room as he started over to pick up the spade again.

The man with the gun was on a nervous edge now and his eyes never left his prisoner, and for that reason he failed to notice where he was placing his boots. When he set one foot without looking on a rock Bannister had thrown out of the hole, it turned and slid under him in the loose dirt and snow. Off balance, Billy Ide glanced hastily at his feet.

And that was all the break that Bannister asked for.

A shift of direction and a lunge carried him against his

108

enemy and they went crashing down together. The gun went off; its roar hammered in Bannister's left ear and set his whole head to ringing, and its flash seemed enough to blind him and set his hair in flames. But his groping left hand closed on the other man's gunwrist, and as they fell he smashed it against the ground with all his strength. He felt the hand open; the gun slid away somewhere and was lost.

Billy Ide, with Bannister half-pinning him down, was squirming and struggling. It was the hard edge of an elbow that struck Bannister along the side of the head, chancing to hit that same tender place where a gunbarrel had knocked him out. Agony bloomed in him. Stunned, blinded by powderflash, he felt himself being kicked and pawed aside as Billy Ide scrambled free of his weight.

By force of will he got to his knees. Raising his head he blinked away the dark afterimage of muzzle flash, focused on the shape of the man standing crouched above him—and saw the knife that had taken the place of the gun in his enemy's hand.

He wouldn't give himself time to think about his dread of that slicing blade. His one hope was to keep moving, keep forcing, before Ide could quite get set and ready. Getting one boot under him he lunged upward. The first he sent lashing at his enemy seemed to lack steam but he felt it lan', glance off. Billy Ide was driven back and Bannister lumbered after him.

Now he struck again, and this time hit solidly. The pale head jerked on its neck and Billy Ide spun half around, slammed full tilt against the side of a boulder and caromed off to the ground.

Bannister, his own head rapidly clearing now, went cautiously after him; but his opponent lay unmoving, face down where he had fallen. Wary, half-suspecting a trick— unable to think he had actually struck that hard—Jim Bannister leaned and caught him by a shoulder, hauled him up roughly.

He almost gagged, as he saw. The collision with the boulder had trapped the blond man's arm and turned the blade of the knife he had held. Falling on it, his own weight had driven the point deep into his belly and up beneath the ribs.

Even as Bannister stared in horror, the knife slid out of the wound and the blood gushed thickly. The dying man gasped and shuddered; the eyes turned back into his head. He went limp, and Bannister let him drop back.

There would be no more knives for Billy Ide.

Jim Bannister had never grown used to the sight of death and the effects of this one, combined with his escape from what had looked like his own sure finish, left him shaken. He let himself down onto a boulder while he had it out.

He nursed the throbbing pain in that hurt left hand, but with all the digging and the fighting there was no fresh blood on the bandage—the knife wound in his palm had not opened again. Later, finding a clean drift of snow, he scooped some up and gingerly touched his throbbing skull with it. That seemed to ease the pounding ache. His throat and mouth felt parched, and he eased them with a couple of handfuls of the snow.

He thought perhaps there might be whiskey in Billy Ide's saddle roll and went to where the horses stood tethered, having settled down again after being startled by that single gunshot; but there was no sign of a bottle.

Bannister was growing steadily stronger, however, and could do without. He found his open gunbelt and holster hooked over the saddlehorn, strapped it in place under the skirt of his blanket coat. His sixshooter was missing, but Billy Ide's gun, he discovered after a moment's search, had slid into the half-dug hole and been nearly buried in a cascade of loose dirt. Bannister went in after it, wiped it clean and dropped it into the holster.

He also found his battered Stetson and drew it on, gingerly. And after that he had no choice but to attack a job that he found extremely distasteful.

It was a temptation to simply roll Billy Ide into that nearby hole and cover him over and leave him, but even Ide deserved a better interment than that. Also, the law would have an interest in his body. So Jim Bannister got the dead man's horse, a rangy buckskin, and led it over and tied it to a bush. He saw the bloody knife again, and with a grimace gave it a hard boot that sent it skittering off across the gully. After that, downing his distaste, he lifted the dead man across the saddle.

The buckskin fidgeted, wanting to bolt from the rank smell of blood, but Bannister got its grisly burden roped securely in place. Afterward, as he sought his own stirrup and caught up the reins of the lead horse, he remembered he was going to have to hunt a way down from here.

He had reached this spot the same way Billy Ide was leaving it—jackknifed across his saddle. He had been unconscious most of the time, and so until he was able to pick up a landmark he did not even know whether Morgan Valley lay to east or west of him. He could do no more than backtrack, following the trail the horses had laid down—a trail, moreover, Ide had no doubt taken every precaution to lose. And, the day was running out.

But it looked as though the man had been careless, or perhaps he was really no expert; if he had tried to hide his tracks he had not managed to do a very good job. Even so, the pressures were on Bannister. The sun had swung over, and already a chill of evening was beginning to flow down from the higher peaks.

By now he had decided that he was in the hills on the western flank of the valley. When finally the crowding rock and timber opened out and he came onto a viewpoint where the whole trough of Morgan Valley lay below him, it swam with blue shadow from the mountain wall behind him while the hills directly across the void shone pearly with dying sun.

He found himself looking anxiously toward Tepee, but intervening hills and timber denied him a view either of the bench where Tate Pauling's headquarters stood, or the threatened stack yard. For all he knew the trap might already have been sprung and the burning had taken place, in which case Grady Sullivan could be dead by now. But he had to assume that it was not true; that in spite of everything there was still time to deliver his warning.

What Billy Ide had told him of his partner's bold scheme

111

to clean out Morgantown by using the keys from the jail desk and making Jim Bannister the scapegoat, was something that would have to wait. At the moment, in contrast with the effort to prevent an ambush killing, it scarcely seemed to matter.

CHAPTER XII

He picked his way down the tough slants until he fell at last into a stock trail that eased the final stretch, bringing him to the valley floor with dusk lying like smoke around him. There he turned northward, still towing the buckskin with its grisly burden.

The trail he was following entered one of the main valley roads, and after that he made better time despite the rapid coming of darkness. Starlight gave some help. The road underfoot was bogged in places by melting snow that was freezing again as the thermometer fell. When he came to a shallow fording of the creek, shore ice crackled under the bays reluctant hoofs but the main channel was clear— fetlock deep and swirling, black and treacherous.

As he rode he peered ahead, anxiously searching but still not catching any hint of fireglow against the thick texture of the darkness. When presently the lights of Tepee headquarters showed, they looked normal enough. He climbed the bench trail and, with the buildings of the ranch compound surrounding him, drew rein.

Everything seemed quiet enough. He was about to ride on to the house when he heard a shout and a man came running across the yard. Bannister waited. On a nearby corral post a lantern swayed in the wind and flung wavering shadows. The Tepee puncher came up, warily circling, peering at the limp form tied across the saddle of the lead horse. "What the hell is this? Who are—?" He recognized the tall man then and grunted, "Bryan. . . ."

112

"I'm looking for Grady Sullivan," Bannister said. "Is he here?"

He got no answer. Two other punchers had come drifting up by this time, and one of them had recognized the dead man's face: "Hell! It's that Billy Ide. You remember, he worked here a while last fall." And the other exclaimed, "My God! Look at the blood! Like somebody gutted him!"

Alive, a man like Ide was not apt to have made any friends among the Tepee crew; but at least these men had known him, and the bloody manner of his death was enough to shock anyone.

The one who had first challenged Bannister was a lantern-jawed man named Dick Flood whom Bannister knew slightly, because he had ridden with the posse that lynched Stella Harbord's husband. Now he demanded, in a voice roughened by shock, "You do this?"

Impatience made Bannister's answer short. "Whether I did or not, it's no concern of yours. I've already said I'm here to see Grady Sullivan. I got a message for him; it's important."

His manner irritated them but something he said must have impressed them, too. Dick Flood scowled and glanced at his companions, but answered grudgingly, "You'll find him at the house. Pauling just now called him over."

"Thanks." Suddenly he was able to pull a deeper breath into his lungs—at least he knew he was in time. But now that that pressure was off he was aware of a letdown feeling and of a dull ache that still remained from the blow he had taken on the skull. With no further word of explanation to Pauling's crewmen he kicked the bay ahead, riding through them, and leading the buckskin on to the main house.

Dismounting, he took the wide steps to the veranda through lamplight falling from the windows. He was about to work the bell knob a second time when the door suddenly swung open and Grady Sullivan himself looked out at him.

The little Irishman exclaimed in surprise, "Bryan! Come in. . ." And as he entered, instinctively ducking the lintel and pulling off his hat, he saw the foreman's eyes narrow. Closing the door, Sullivan raked his long frame with a glance. "Man, what have you been tangling with?"

113

Bannister knew he must be a sight. His clothing muddy, fouled with Billy Ide's blood as well as his own. But for the moment he shrugged the question aside. He looked through a wide doorway where he could see the back of Tate Pauling's massive head and hunched shoulders as the rancher sat at table, wolfing down something that smelled from where he stood like beef stew.

Grady Sullivan must have guessed somehow that the visitor's belly was grinding on emptiness, for he said quickly, "You eaten? Come on in and fill a plate for yourself."

But Bannister shook his head. "That can wait. And I got news that won't! It looks like you may have been right," he went on, "when you told me your neighbors were planning open war. Because, according to what I hear, you can be expecting a call from them almost any minute."

The Irishman stared. "I don't follow you. . ."

"What I hear is, Rickman and some of the others are going after your stack yard—with a torch!"

"Now? Tonight?" The exclamation burst from him. As Bannister nodded there was the heavy scrape of a chair turning and Tate Pauling's voice boomed at them from within the dining room.

"What the devil's going on in there?"

Pauling was craned around in his chair, glowering at them. He looked very much as he had two days ago, at the time of Bannister's Sunday visit. He was dressed this time but needed a shave, and his graying shock of hair was an uncombed wild tangle in the lamplight. "I hear you talking, behind my back," he said heavily. "Come here, will you? I want to know what's up."

"It's nothing, Mister Pauling," the foreman tried to explain, but his employer cut him off, with a sweep of the hand.

"Damn it, I said come in here!"

Grady Sullivan gave the visitor a look of apology, tempered by patience. Jim Bannister started to say quickly, "Wait a minute! There's more I haven't told you. . ." But the foreman had already started away from him.

Bannister slapped his hat against his leg in irritation, and followed him into the dining room. The big table could have seated a dozen, but there was only one place set. A coffeepot, bowls of stew, and fresh-baked biscuits sent up a tempting aroma.

Tate Pauling had pushed his plate aside now, and with elbows propped on the table was holding a cup half-filled with black coffee between his hands. The hands shook slightly. Jim Bannister wondered if possibly he had a bottle under the table that he was using in the coffee when his foreman was not watching.

He said again, "Now, what the hell's going on?"

"A little matter that's come up, Mister Pauling," the foreman said. "Nothing to bother you with—I'll take care of it."

"Before I forget," Bannister put in, "I got your friend Billy Ide outside, there, tied on his horse. I'd like to leave him with you, if I could."

The men both turned on him. Sullivan exclaimed, "You mean—he's dead?"

"As dead as he'll ever be, and not a very pretty sight either. It was a sort of accident—he fell on his own knife."

There were plates on the sideboard. As the two men stared, Bannister took a plate and spooned beef stew onto it, added a couple of biscuits. He filled a thick china mug from the coffeepot and, standing there, began to eat; the grub tasted as good as it smelled. He said, "It's too long a story to tell now, but I've been hauling him around with me for the past few hours and it's getting to be a nuisance. I've got still more riding to do. I'd appreciate it if you'd let me leave him on ice here until it's decided what should be done with him."

"I'll have the boys tend to it," Grady promised, and turned to leave.

"Stand still, damn it!" Tate Pauling slammed his cup down, slopping its contents; a dark brown stain began to spread over the tablecloth. The rancher swung a look between the two men standing before him. "You think I'm too stupid to know when I'm being put off? Now, somebody better start talking!"

Grady Sullivan settled his shoulders. He looked at

Bannister above his employer's head, drew a breath. "All right, Mister Pauling," he said. "Jim Bryan, here, is of the opinion somebody may be planning to burn off our feed stacks."

Pauling's massive head jerked; his eyes flickered with surprise and anger. "Like hell they are!"

"He thinks Gil Rickman's the leader."

The smoky eyes lifted to Bannister. "And just where did you get this?"

"I prefer not to say," Bannister replied, calmly working on his plate of grub. "But I think it's on the level."

Tate Pauling swore. He put up a hand, wiped the palm across his mouth and heavy mustache. To Grady Sullivan, Bannister said, "There's still a little more to this. The feed stacks aren't really the main target. *You* are."

"Me?" The Irishman blinked in pure astonishment.

He nodded. "Some of that crowd don't know it yet, but the real idea behind the thing is to pull you into a trap. There'll be shooting, and in the confusion they hope to finish you off. They figure that's how they can damage Tepee the worst." He added: "I imagine they're not far from right."

"I see. . . ." The Irishman's broad face, with its battered nose, looked gravely thoughtful. Though he was a modest man, he must have seen the truth of the argument. For all his arrogant bluster, without his foreman to lean on Tate Pauling could now hardly carry on a fight against the enemies he had made for himself. There had been too much deterioration, too many months of hard and endless drinking and general letting go. Tate Pauling was simply in no shape to take command of his own affairs.

Grady Sullivan shifted his boots. "Well," he said, "whatever happens, we can't lose our feed reserves—not even if this thaw should last. Tepee just can't afford to let anyone do a thing like this and get away with it.

"I'll go tell the boys to saddle and be ready to ride."

"Hold on, there!" He had reached the doorway when Tate Pauling's deep voice halted him. "Aren't you even waiting to hear your orders?"

Sullivan slowly turned. He said without expression, "Yes, Mister Pauling?"

The chair scraped as the rancher pushed himself to his feet. The way he caught at its back to steady himself was all Bannister needed to tell him that Pauling had indeed been drinking; he probably would not have been able to sit a saddle, but his arrogance and authority were undiminished.

"You don't seem to understand," he said, "that the marshal here has given us an opportunity we may never see again. Now we got a chance for a little surprise of our own—to make damn sure none of that crowd rides to threaten Tepee again!"

Bannister saw that hit the foreman, saw the Irishman's stare slowly widen. "You ain't saying—?"

"You got ears!" Tate Pauling raised a fist and brought it crashing down on the table beside him, making the dishes jump and chime. "It's no time to be squeamish. These bastards are raiding *us*! We're only defending our own ground—and we're in our rights to wipe out the whole kit and boiling of them. Do you understand me?"

Grady Sullivan swallowed. And then his honest, stubborn Irish face went hard and his shoulders settled. "I understand," he said, and walked out of the house.

Face wooden, Jim Bannister dropped his fork into his plate and laid it on the table. In the heavy stillness he demanded harshly, "I hope you realize what you've just ordered that man to do!"

Slowly the massive head turned to him. Muddy eyes containing a flicker of anger regarded him coldly. Tate Pauling lifted one hand, a shade unsteadily, and a finger stabbed at Bannister.

"And, by God, he'll do it! He's never yet refused an order from me. If you don't like it—it's my ranch, Bryan; not even the law can say a thing about the method I choose to protect my property. Deny me that, if you can!"

Bannister picked up the hat he had laid aside. He did not try to keep the contempt from his voice. "I guess you'll never really change, will you? Nothing can teach you—it wouldn't matter, in the long run, how many innocent men might come to be lynched because of you! You're a ruthless and arrogant man, and you'll be one to the end. I only wonder how long a good man like Grady Sullivan can be fooled into doing your will."

The other glared at him, breathing heavily. Out in the yard, men could be heard yelling in busy excitement. Boots slapped the earth; at the corral a horse whinnied shrilly as it was roped. Tate Pauling said, "Get out of my house!"

CHAPTER XIII

Grady Sullivan had remembered his promise to dispose of Billy Ide. Both the dead man and his mount had been moved from where Bannister left them, and he found only the bay waiting for him. Relieved to be freed of the lead horse and its burden, he swung into saddle and started for the trail down off the bench.

At the corral yonder, Pauling's crew was nearly ready to ride. Drawing rein a moment, Bannister watched the mill of men and horses by the streaky light of the lantern that swung on the corral post; hearing their excited voices, the thud of hoofs, and the popping of leather. He counted almost a dozen riders.

Now a puncher came at a run from the bunkhouse carrying a filled belt, holster, and rifle which he passed up to Grady Sullivan and afterward hurried to his own saddle. The foreman shoved the rifle into his saddle boot, strapped the handgun around his middle.

They were all equally well armed, Bannister saw with grim disapproval. Still it was ultimately none of his business. He shook his head and booted the gelding, angrily.

At the foot of the bench trail he heard the crew come bearing after him, and pulled aside to let them storm by. Sullivan was in the lead, setting a hard pace. The bay caught the infection of excitement, and wanted to fall in, but Bannister held it under a firm hand and watched as the clot of riders stretched out across the flats and pointed toward the threatened stack yard. Afterward he reined in the other direction, himself taking the road to Morgantown.

But he had gone less than a dozen yards when he suddenly yanked rein. The baffled horse circled uneasily while its rider craned to hear the fading sound of those Tepee horsemen. "Oh, hell!" Bannister said under his breath. With a shrug of resignation he went spurring directly after them.

They had not got much of a lead, and the bay quickly cut it down. Very shortly the dark clot of horsemen showed just ahead of him and then he was bursting into their midst, shouting Grady Sullivan's name. The Irishman answered in a voice heavy with suspicion.

"What do you want?"

"I'm riding with you."

"The hell you are!" But Bannister would not turn back and he would not argue. He simply fell in beside the leader and so they rode, for awhile, in a hostile stillness that was something almost tangible—until at last the Irishman exploded.

"Damn it, what do you think you're doing? You brought us the word, for which I'm grateful. But you got no part in this business; I want you out of it! Like Mister Pauling said, it's a private fight—and we're on our own ground. We're in our rights."

"I heard what Mister Pauling said," Bannister answered coldly. "I didn't think much of it!"

The foreman's reply was uncompromising. "It don't matter a damn what you thought of it, Bryan! Mister Pauling gives the orders on Tepee—and if I'm able, I carry them out!"

"Even this kind of an order? My God, man! Have you actually stopped to consider what he wants done to those neighbors of his?"

"They started it!"

"And this will sure as hell finish it!" He was pressing hard, almost despairing of making any dent in such blind stubbornness. "Loyalty is one thing, Sullivan—but it's murder he's asking for! And you're too good a man to let yourself be used for such a purpose!"

119

A cry broke from the rider beside him. "Will you shut up?" Sullivan's sudden, convulsive jerk at the reins flung his mount's head high. His free hand shot across the distance between their saddles, clutching Bannister's shoulder with a grip the latter felt even through the heavy material of his coat. It was almost as though the man would try to haul him, by sheer force, from his saddle.

The foreman cried in a voice that shook, "Will you let me do my job?"

"The real question is," Jim Bannister retorted coolly, "will your conscience let you?"

What Sullivan might have said to that was lost as an exclamation broke, without warning, from one of his followers: "Grady! *Look!*"

Everyone saw it: A spot of brightness, like a star fallen to the floor of the valley a couple miles ahead of them. They each understood what it was.

Grady Sullivan swore, and his hand fell away from Bannister's shoulder, but it didn't take his yell to send the lot of them spurring forward again—digging a gallop from their horses in spite of the treacherous darkness and the uneven ground.

That twinkling point of flame disappeared behind a dip in the land, and when it appeared again seemed already to have grown to twice its size. Now a second one joined it, as another stack of cut feed took the torch. Still, if the real purpose was to lure their intended victim and give light enough to target him, Bannister thought the attackers would have to be careful not to burn out all the stacks at once.

He was about to demand a halt when Grady Sullivan, on his own account, ordered the men to pull up.

As their horses blew and stirred restlessly the foreman said, "There's no sense riding straight into their sights. If it's a trap, looks to me they'll be holed up in the timber below that ridge just to the west."

Bannister asked, "Can we get around them?"

"We should be able to—by coming in across the rise at their backs. I can see," the Irishman added, with a grudging respect, "that you and I are thinking along the same line."

"Since they've baited the trap," Bannister suggested

120

bluntly, "maybe you'd best rebait it. Send in a couple of your boys to do what they can about putting those fires out. That should keep our friends occupied, and without running too much risk. If they're really waiting for you, they won't likely open up on anyone else until you've shown."

Sullivan appeared to like that, for he turned at once to give the order. Dick Flood and two others quickly volunteered for the ticklish job of acting as decoys, and the foreman accepted them. A few last-minute instructions and he sent them on, the rest of the party moving out shortly afterward.

The blazing stacks were now close enough so that they could almost see the flames whipping in the wind, and the sparks streaming. Presently, behind Sullivan's lead, the horsemen dropped into a gully that broke away at an angle and deepened as they rode—at a walk now, with half-frozen mud and snow crunching underfoot.

Jim Bannister kept his silence. This was Sullivan's show, and for the moment he was grimly concerned in standing by and watching to see what the Tepee foreman did with it. But presently a movement just ahead brought a quick warning from him, and Sullivan called a halt as starlight revealed the stir of a clot of saddled horses tied in scrub timber.

Grady Sullivan grunted in satisfaction. "We're guessing right so far—here's their animals. From here we go afoot."

Dismounting to anchor his reins, Bannister saw the Irishman pull the rifle from his saddle boot, and with a quick movement lever a shell into the breech. His face went a little bleak at that, but he made no comment.

Now a word brought the crew gathering around their foreman. Sullivan gestured toward the timbered rise beside them. "Go easy," he warned. "Don't bunch up, but keep in touch. They should be just beyond this ridge."

It was no easy matter to climb silently, with no light except the stars, but the men of Tepee did well enough. Bannister, picking his own way over slick rock and slippery mud and through brush and jackpine, could hear from time to time the small sounds of the skirmish line—the rattle of brush, and a scrape of bootleather, the occasional sound of a gunbutt striking rock, or someone's muffled curse as he

121

snagged his clothing and tore loose. But for the most part they managed to maintain quiet, and the normal night noises and the wash of wind in the treeheads likely covered them.

Past the crest the ridge seemed to be less heavily timbered, ribbed by granite outcroppings. A whispered order came along to hold the men where they were, momentarily; but Bannister continued to move forward and so came upon Grady Sullivan, settled in a nest of rock that commanded the lower skirt of the slope. The Irishman turned, startled, then gave a grunt as Bannister identified himself.

"See anything?"

"Plenty," the foreman whispered. "There they are!"

Through the ranks of pencil-thin jackpine a glow from burning hay stacks—several of them now in flames—made black bars of the tree trunks. Almost at once Bannister picked out the silhouette of a man, nearly shapeless in his heavy coat and steepled hat. He offered an easy target as he crouched motionless beside a tree bole, still unaware of any danger at his back.

From beyond the fringe of trees a crackling of flames could be heard, and the voices of the Pauling crewmen as they moved about the fenced feed yard—working at the blazing stacks, trying to tear them apart and scatter them so as to save the unburnt centers. The ambushers were watching, but also waiting; obviously they still hoped for a chance at their primary target—Grady Sullivan.

Bannister drew a breath. "All right," he told the man beside him. "This is what you planned on. We've got position; they're between us and the fires. You can probably wipe them all out without much trouble. You know how Tate Pauling would see it. He'd say it's always easiest to kill an enemy when you've got him, unknowing, with his back turned. . . ."

"*Damn you, Bryan!*" The foreman's voice shook with anger and indecision.

"Well, you better make up your mind."

He almost thought, under the goading, that the man was going to hit him—he stiffened, prepared for it. But Grady

122

Sullivan turned away, eased to his feet, and suddenly his shout cut across the stillness:

"Rickman? Pitts?" Bannister could imagine the effect of it hitting the unsuspecting men below. He saw the man he had been watching freeze in the act of turning.

"Listen to me!" the Irishman continued. "All of you! This is Grady Sullivan speaking. We've got you pinned—and for what you've done here I'd be in my rights to order you shot where you stand. But I won't, if you'll get rid of your guns and surrender!"

There was an outbreak of startled talk down there. Finally Gil Rickman's challenge came—a harsh shout: "You're bluffing!"

"You think so?" Sullivan retorted. "Show them, boys. Give them a shot—just over their heads!"

His own sixgun fired the signal, and on the instant lances of flame and a startling racket of gunfire rolled along the slope. Bannister, using the weapon taken from Billy Ide, put a bullet past the silhouette and saw the man fall away from it, frantically. Into the echoes of the volley someone cried, in a voice on the verge of hysteria: "Oh, my God!"

"You can have more," Sullivan warned. "Only, next time, we won't be shooting into the trees. Or would you rather throw away your guns and move down off this hill, into the open?"

No answer, for a moment. Bannister knew Gil Rickman must be talking fast, arguing, trying hard to hold the rest in line. But these were not fighters, and their nerve could not survive such stretching.

Suddenly one called up: "Can you hear me? Don't shoot! I'm throwing it down!"

Sullivan gave a grunt of satisfaction. "I think that does it," he said. An order sent his riders forward.

Immediately, with the first break, all resistance crumbled. In another moment, for all of Rickman's cursing and shouting, men were stumbling empty-handed into the open. The Tepee crew came down off the slope and through the last of the trees, sweeping the prisoners before them.

Dick Flood and the other pair of Tepee riders had succeeded by now in putting out all but one blazing stack that

123

was too far gone; that wind-whipped torch served for illumination.

They outnumbered their captors. Looking at the frightened faces, Jim Bannister recognized most of those he had seen at Rickman's on Sunday. And yes, there was Rickman himself—sullen and defiant, but apparently recognizing that this fight, at least, was lost.

Bannister searched for Ira Stiegel, but failed to find him. True to his declared intention, Stiegel had simply failed to show. Stiegel was certainly no hero and, in fact, he had betrayed his friends. Still, he had only tried to do what he believed was right. . . .

Most of the prisoners were frightened and bewildered, but Gil Rickman was furious. He discovered Bannister among the ring of captors and exclaimed belligerently, "Bryan! I guess now we know what you were really up to, that afternoon at my place when you claimed your horse needed shoeing. Hell! You're nothing but a damn spy for Tate Pauling!"

Bannister shrugged. Let Rickman think what he liked; it would help draw suspicion away from Ira Stiegel. Grady Sullivan, looking at the men he had taken prisoner, said heavily, "You people have really piled up a case against yourselves: Trespassing, destruction of property, attempted murder—"

"*Murder!*" Someone echoed in protest, his voice breaking on the word; and Rickman shouted, "You're crazy!"

"You deny this was meant to be an ambush?"

"Of course I deny it! And these men will bear me out."

Jim Bannister shrugged. "Dave Pitts was the only one in on the scheme. How about it, Pitts? Which of you was to put the bullet into Sullivan? Or were you both going to have a try, to make sure of him?"

The man seemed to recoil. He cast a look around, seeing all their eyes on him and no escape. "Now, wait a minute!" he stammered. "You can't pin this on me. It was Rickman's idea!"

The Bear Paw owner let out a roar. Before anyone could stop him he lunged at the other rancher and a wild swing of his fist smashed Pitts in the face, sending him staggering. He would have struck again, except that one of the captors grabbed his shoulder and hurled him back.

Bannister, seeing the looks of bewilderment and dawning horror on the rest of the captives, felt a suspicion turn somehow to dead certainty. Even though he had no proof in such a moment, with the enemy caught off balance, a bluff would serve. He said coldly, "I don't think it was all Rickman's idea. Gil, why don't you tell us why you went to see Claude Youngdahl yesterday morning—was that when you received your orders?"

"What are you talking about?" The man shouted it at him. "I wasn't at Youngdahl's."

"It's no use lying," Bannister warned him—and having done so, blandly added a lie of his own: "You were seen."

That stopped the man for an instant, his mouth agape. He swallowed. "Well—and what of it?" he retorted. "The bank holds paper against my spread—like most of the other outfits. I went up to talk about an extension. Nothing wrong with that, I reckon."

"Then why deny it?" Bannister persisted. "And why sneak out the back way, while Youngdahl was letting me in the front? Maybe it never occurred to you that Youngdahl was going to talk to me quite as free as he did."

"Oh?" Rickman's head appeared to settle a trifle between his shoulders—like a fighter setting himself for a blow. "What did he say?"

"He said plenty! He offered me Sam White's job, plus a hundred dollars a month out of his own pocket if I'd run the office to satisfy *him*. He said the day was soon coming when he'd be the one big man in Morgan Valley."

This much was the truth. Now came the part composed of pure bluff and guesswork: "He told me your job was to get rid of Grady Sullivan, and leave Tate Pauling without a foreman to fight his battles. After all, Pauling is one man he's never been able to get his hooks into. But once your crowd had smashed Tepee and divided it among themselves, Youngdahl figured there'd be plenty of time to finish them off separately—end up, eventually, taking over all of Morgan Valley."

Rickman's voice was tight and trembling. "Supposing
125

there was any truth in this! Can you tell me any reason why I'd want any part in such a plan?"

"I imagine you've got your price," Jim Bannister answered. "Youngdahl's no rancher. If he converts the valley into a cattle empire, he's going to be needing someone to run it. That should be bait enough for you, since you know you stand to lose your spread to him anyway. And, it wouldn't cost him anything to make the offer, even if he meant to back out on his promise. . . ."

Stung, Rickman shouted, "Damn you! He wouldn't dare!" And then stood aghast, as he realized what had tumbled from his lips.

Jim Bannister turned to the rest of the prisoners. "There's your answer," he said.

CHAPTER XIV

The hay stack had burnt itself out. Now only the stars, reflected faintly by patches of unmelted snow, gave what light there was. After a moment, Grady Sullivan's stocky figure stirred in the darkness; his voice was gruff. "Your broncs are where you left them," he told the prisoners. "Take 'em and get out of here. All of you!"

Contrite and punished by the knowledge of the way they had let themselves be duped, they seemed unable to believe they were being let off so lightly. They neither argued nor wasted time. Without a word they went moving off into the trees—all but Gil Rickman, for Grady Sullivan halted him with a harsh grunt. "Not quite all of you! Not you, mister! Not so damned fast!"

The man squared himself, facing the Irishman across the barrel of the rifle glinting faintly in the other's hands. "What are you going to do with me?"

"You know any good reason I shouldn't just plug you where you stand?" Bannister and the Tepee crew waited; the very night seemed to be stilled. Then the foreman let out his breath in a tired expletive. "Oh, hell! Get out of here. Run and tell Youngdahl it's no go. But, by God, don't ever let me lay eyes on you again!"

Without a word, Gil Rickman turned and walked away. The trees swallowed him.

Grady Sullivan turned to his men. "Some of you go make sure that crowd really leaves without any tricks. And fetch us back our horses." As they moved away on this assignment he turned to Dick Flood. "What was the damage?"

It had not been too great, apparently. Only one stack was completely gone, with three others partly burnt before the Tepee crewmen had been able to scatter the fires. Sullivan heard the report without comment.

To Jim Bannister, the Irishman's manner seemed strangely withdrawn and preoccupied. He sensed no triumph in the man, no satisfaction over a difficult job well handled. Bannister ventured a comment of his own: "I don't know how Tate Pauling's going to like it, but I think you did the right thing just now. Those neighbors of yours should have learned a lesson. At least they won't be blindly following after Rickman and Youngdahl soon again."

With an effort Sullivan seemed to pull himself out of his strange and moody thoughts. "You were the one that brought this off. I wish I knew how much you really knew about that pair, and how much you were guessing."

"It was mostly guessing," Bannister admitted. "And a good percentage of bluff. But I figured my guesses were right."

"They were close enough to split that bastard Rickman wide open. As for the rest—this should knock the fight out of them for a long time to come!"

Presently the horses were brought up, together with a report that the raiders were scattering without further argument. Jim Bannister, with other unfinished business already nagging at him, waited to hear little of this. He tested the bay's cinch and had just mounted when Grady Sullivan strode toward him. "You're not coming back to Tepee?"

"I'm needed in town."

127

"Wish you could be there when Mister Pauling hears what happened. A war could have started tonight. Instead you stopped it cold. The credit should go where it belongs. For one, I'd like to thank you."

Bannister saw the hand he extended. He reached down, took it briefly. "Glad I could help," he said, "but I'm not sure Tate Pauling would agree. We didn't exactly carry out his orders."

Grady Sullivan was oddly silent at that. Getting no answer, Bannister nodded and picked up the reins. "See you," he grunted and put the bay in motion.

For a long moment after he had gone Grady Sullivan stood unmoving, staring into the dark. Dick Flood, bringing his horse, had to speak twice before the Irishman seemed to hear: "Ready?" Like a man coming out of a trance, Sullivan moved his shoulders and mumbled something as he took the reins and turned to hunt stirrup.

That same strange brooding hung over him during the return ride to headquarters, contrasting with the noisy jubilation of the crew now that the tension of danger was lifted. On the bench he did not ride with them to unsaddle at the corral, nor did he head for the main house.

Instead he made directly toward the bunkshack, where a tiny room partitioned at one end of the long log structure was all the home he had known in the years he had rodded Tepee. He left his horse standing on thrown reins as he entered.

When, minutes later, he blew out the lamp he had lit and stepped outside again with a blanket roll under his arm Tate Pauling was waiting for him.

The lantern on the corral post threw a dim and streaky light upon them. It made the eyes in Pauling's blocky face appear cavernous.

"Well?" the rancher snapped. "What's the idea leaving me to set over there at the house, waiting for your report? You forgotten I have some slight interest in whatever it was happened tonight?"

"I hadn't forgotten," the Irishman said calmly. "I was coming—as soon as I finished here." He slung his blanket roll behind the saddle of his waiting horse, and began to lash

128

it in place with the leather strings. Tate Pauling watched his movements for a moment, then burst forth with an explosion of sound that echoed around the ranch yard.

"Just what the hell do you think you're doing?"

"What's it look like? I'm leaving."

"*Leaving*?"

Grady Sullivan tied down hard, tested the knot, and then reached across his horse's rump for the opposite tie-strings. "I'm leaving you, Tate," he repeated. It was the first time he had ever called this man by any name other than the formal, respectful "Mister Pauling."

"I can't work for you any more—not after tonight. It couldn't ever again be like what it was."

"I wish I knew what this nonsense is you're talking!"

Still working with the knots, the Irishman answered solemnly: "A lot of years I've ridden for you, and I was proud to do it. The day you named me your foreman was about the finest day of my life. You ain't been the easiest man to work for, Tate. You've treated me pretty much like a dog at times. But I've taken your bad manners and your insolence because I respected you, and figured them for the signs of a great man. What's more, until tonight I've not refused to take any order you ever gave me. If your memory's any good, you should know that."

Scowling, Tate Pauling admitted grudgingly, "You been a good enough foreman. Did I ever say otherwise?"

"You never said anything," Sullivan retorted, swinging about to face him. "Certainly, one thing you never said was, 'Thanks!' But that ain't what I'm talking about," he went on, as the other made an irritable gesture. "None of this matters at all, any more. It sure as hell ain't the reason I'm leaving, or I'd have left a long time ago!

"Tonight, when you ordered me to do murder—that was the end! You've always fought hard, and you've fought rough; but you never before handed me *that* kind of assignment. You've gone a long way down, Tate, farther than I realized.

"During these last months I tried to make allowances on account of what happened to Meg; I watched you fall apart and hoped you'd pull yourself together. But tonight I see

129

you ain't worth anybody's loyalty—and likely never were."

Tate Pauling stared at him. Finally he said, "I think I know what's eating you! You been listening to that tall bastard—that fellow Bryan!" The name sounded like an obscenity.

Sullivan wagged his head. "Maybe—just in time—I have! He was there with me. We stood off your enemies, together, and we pulled their fangs. So for the time being, at least, you're safe. I'm leaving Tepee in good shape.

"But if they ever crowd you again you'll have to fight them alone, or else find yourself another boy. I'm through with you and I'm through with Morgan Valley. I don't like the smell of this range . . . all of a sudden I want out."

He turned to his horse, then, and deliberately swung astride. With the reins in his hands, he looked again at this man he had served. His voice held a note of sadness. "It's been a lot of years, Tate. And a lot of them were pretty good. For them, you got my thanks. Too bad I had to go and lose my faith in you, and my respect for you."

"Go to hell, then!" growled Tate Pauling, coarsely, unrelenting to the end. And as he watched Grady Sullivan ride away from Tepee, for the last time, he made no attempt to call him back.

Virg Clausen was having his troubles. So far nothing—absolutely nothing—had worked out according to program, and his mood grew steadily more savage under the raw pressures of danger and disappointment.

Following his original plan, he was working his way down from the head of the gulch street toward an abandoned mine adit in the slope behind the Dutchman's where his horse was waiting under saddle, in case he had to make a hurried getaway.

The keys from the jail desk—each with its identifying tag—had been carefully sorted and arranged in order on a loop of cotton string to eliminate fumbling for each one as he wanted it. Every detail had been thought out carefully.

It was infuriating to watch everything go wrong.

The first building he had entered was Lloyd Canby's

130

general store, which he had expected to pass up because he knew Canby lived in the building. But the store was dark, and finally satisfied that its owner was gone—probably off somewhere with his poker-playing cronies on the town council—Clausen took a chance and let himself in.

It was pitch dark, of course, but with an occasional light from a block of sulphur matches he picked a way through the cluttered storeroom to the counter. The cash drawer had a flimsy lock, which he broke with a thrust of the file he had brought with him. Inside the drawer he found fifteen dollars in coins and crumpled bills.

Clausen swore, even as he was scooping out the money and thrusting it into a pocket of his coat. The match burned down and he dropped it, and stood in the dark wondering where, if not here, Canby kept his ready cash. In his living quarters, perhaps, at the rear?

He prowled his way back there, lit more matches, and found all the bleak clutter of a bachelor's world. But though he probed about—jerking open drawers and emptying them, and even pawing through the clothing that hung behind a curtain in a corner of the room—he could discover no hiding place here for money. Cursing, he abandoned the search.

In quick succession he knocked off two more businesses—a harness shop, and Joe Ries's drugstore. In the former he discovered no money whatsoever, though he did see a leather quirt that struck his fancy and helped himself to that for lack of better spoils. The till at the drug store yielded an exact total of seven dollars and thirty-two cents.

He now began to suspect what he supposed he ought to have guessed in the first place: There was very little ready cash floating about Morgantown at this dead end of winter. Except at places like the barber shop or the restaurant or the town's saloons, it began to look as though people here bought their goods on tick and paid for them in a general settling of accounts during roundup and market season. If so, that meant he had only one hope at all of leaving with the kind of stake he had envisioned; and now he crouched out in

131

the darkness and, without much hope, studied the blocky mass of Claude Youngdahl's bank.

Early in the game he had crossed the bank off his list. Youngdahl, in raising his building, had installed a gleaming, impregnable-looking vault that was a discouragement to anyone who knew as little as Virg Clausen did about safecracking.

But now he found himself reconsidering, for through the lighted windows he could see somebody at work in there—Youngdahl's clerk, a cowed, bent-shouldered fellow named Farley. The man was seated at his high bookkeeper's desk, patiently toiling over a ledger. He was all alone.

A side door opened into Youngdahl's dark, partitioned office; and a key to that door was in Virg Clausen's hand. He fingered it, scowling in agonized uncertainty. But finally, his decision made, he rose and moved forward to the side of the bank and then along the wall and under the eaves where meltwater dripped occasionally into the puddles below. He reached the door, fitted the key and felt the action of the lock turn over. In another moment he was inside and cautiously closing the door again behind him.

A dim pencilstroke of light outlined the inner office door; a single struck match aided him in avoiding the flat-topped desk that occupied the center of the room. He drew his gun and, holding it, found the knob and turned it with painful care.

The metal parts ground under his hand and the sound of it seemed to fill the darkness. Then the door inched open to give him a view of the clerk's bent shoulders under the bracket lamp on the wall above his desk. The big face of the vault gleamed dully at the end of the room. The rasp of Farley's busy pen was the only sound.

Clausen shoved the door wide. Deliberately roughening his voice to disguise it, he said, "Freeze! Turn your head, and you're a dead man!"

The figure on the high stool jerked violently. The pen dropped and rolled clattering down the slanted desk and to the floor. "Who—who is it?" the clerk stammered. "What do you want?"

"Never mind who it is. Just get down off that stool and

132

back toward me. Don't turn! Keep your eyes on the wall, and both hands where I can see them!"

The man hastily obeyed. But he had enough spirit to give a warning as he came off the stool: "Whoever you are you're making a mistake! There's nothing here for you. And whatever you've got in mind doing, this town is too small to hide you afterward."

Clausen answered in that same altered voice: "Let me worry about it. This lousy town has done me dirt, and I'm getting out of it—tonight. Now, you hold still!" A step brought him behind the other, and as the gun shoved deep into his ribs the clerk went rigid, arms jerking higher, breath sucking in audibly.

With a quick movement Clausen passed a hand over the man's clothing. Not finding a weapon he stepped back, grunting his satisfaction. "All right," he said. "Open the vault."

"Do *what*?" It was almost a bleat. Involuntarily the man started to turn but Clausen struck his shoulder hard with the flat of a hand, to remind him. "But—I can't!"

"Think again!" A vicious shove sent Farley stumbling in the direction of the vault. "And don't tempt me."

Driven ahead of him, the trembling clerk shook his head in protest at every step. "You don't understand!" he cried, tremulously. "I mean, I really can't. Once the timelock's been set there's no power on earth will open it till morning."

Clausen felt a crawl of sick disappointment, and then a brutal anger took over. "You're lying!" he cried hoarsely.

"No—it's true! I swear! You can kill me, but it won't do you any good!"

"I said, quit lying!" the redhead shouted. Then, controlling his temper long enough to remember the part he was playing, he deliberately added, "I killed a man last night for less than this. Don't think I won't do it again!"

The clerk halted dead in his tracks. "You killed a man?" he repeated. It seemed to hit him, then. "My God!" he cried suddenly. "Are you *Bryan*?" And, as though astonishment wiped out all caution he jerked about. He was an ineffectual little man, with blinking eyes and a balding scalp blotched with freckles. A ludicrous expression came over him as he

133

saw, instead of the one he expected, the face of Virg Clausen. His mouth opened; his throat swelled as though on the beginning of a shout.

It never came, for in the same instant a savage impulse dropped the trigger under Clausen's splayed thumb. The roar of the revolver smashed against the walls and the bank's low ceiling. The clerk was flung bodily by the impact of the point-blank shot, to strike the teller's cage and drop like a rag doll with a smear of red quickly forming across his shirtfront.

Choking on powder smoke, and with his head ringing from the punishing concussion, Virg Clausen could only stare at the man he had shot. It was only when he heard the first faint outcry, somewhere in the night, that he really comprehended what he had done. And then the pressure was on him.

He threw a last bitter, baffled stare at the closed vault, now that any chance at what it contained was lost. He cursed, turned, and fled.

He left the doors standing open, hardly aware of what he was doing until he found himself outside in the night and standing with shoulders pressed against the damp wall of an adjoining building. There he listened to the drip from the eaves, hearing beyond that the growing, startled sound as Morgantown came alive. A door slammed, and then another. Voices threw questions back and forth; the trampling of boots sounded on sidewalk planks, then drew nearer.

Clausen turned and moved back from the street, circling the dark rear of the building. Debating briefly, he told himself there was really nothing to run from—and no place to run if he wanted to, in this clutter of half-abandoned buildings that called itself a town. Now that all his schemes had been blown to hell the best recourse was to boldness.

All at once he realized he was still carrying the gun. Hastily punching out the used shell and replacing it from his belt loops, he holstered the weapon and then walked forward again to the street. Here, men were rushing by; excitement was swelling. Virg Clausen called out to someone: "What's going on?"

The man threw an answer across his shoulder. "Didn't

134

you hear the shot? Somebody said the bank's been robbed!"

A bunch of men went by at a run, jostling him against the wall. It occurred to Virg Clausen then that he could not afford to seem too indifferent. So, even though reluctant, he shrugged and fell in with the current and let it carry him once more in the direction of the bank.

Someone had discovered the unlocked side door. The crowd pushed through, shoving Claude Youngdahl's desk aside as they trampled across the darkened office. Out in the main room, though, there was stillness. Past the heads that crowded the doorway, Clausen looked in at the intent and motionless group standing about the man lying on the floor in his own blood.

Suddenly it was as though icy fingers reached into Virg Clausen's chest and stopped his heart from beating.

Farley had been raised so that his head and shoulders leaned against the front of the teller's cage. He sprawled there looking more dead than alive—but he was not dead. Not yet. The eyes in his bloodless face glistened in the lamplight and his lips were moving. A painful, halting whisper made the stillness ache with the effort behind it.

Nausea shook Clausen as he realized he had failed to make sure the bullet had done its work. Next moment he wheeled and began fighting a way through the men crowding behind him. They cursed him, but let him through. He was almost in a frenzy when he finally broke through and gained the open, and the fresh darkness outside.

In a matter of minutes, he knew they'd be after him. Alone, and for the moment unobserved, he wasted no more time. He ran.

Crouching just within the mouth of the abandoned adit with his horse stomping restlessly behind him, Virg Clausen clutched his gun and waited while his enemies scoured the gulch for him. He could almost smell the sour sweat of fear on himself, despite the night's chill.

He watched bobbing lanterns move among the houses, hearing from time to time the querulous call of voices. The few words he could make out had already told him Farley was dead of his chest wound. Now Morgantown was out for blood. More than once Clausen heard his own name, and each time it made him shudder.

Even with that stupid Bert Dakins leading the manhunt, they could not blunder about like this forever. Sooner or later, someone was going to think of checking these abandoned mines dotting the slopes above the gulch. Well, when they came at this one—Clausen promised himself grimly—they would pay a high price for taking him. The lousy bastards!

He hated everyone, just then: That damned bank clerk for forcing him to shoot; Claude Youngdahl for having all the money in Morgantown locked up in a vault that could not be broken; even his own partner, Billy Ide, who was waiting somewhere safe, right now, after his easy and pleasant assignment of getting rid of the yellow-haired marshal.

The only satisfaction lay in knowing that that Bryan son of a bitch would at least have got what was coming to him. It was small enough consolation. . . .

Clausen's head jerked as a man shouted, somewhere farther up the street: "Here! This way! *I see him!*" At once other voices took up the cry, like hounds on a scent.

Clausen's brow puckered and he stepped out into the open; for a moment he stood there in pure puzzlement, watching a tide of sparks that were carried lanterns suddenly go streaming up the slant of the gulch. It took him a moment to guess what must have happened—and then suddenly he was grinning, his cheeks stretching under their stubble of unshaved beard.

By God, if they weren't hot on a wrong trail! He wouldn't be surprised if it was Dakins himself that had panicked at his own shadow and thrown the whole manhunt off!

It was all the chance he needed, and perhaps the only one he would have. In another moment he was leading the horse, a dun gelding, out into the open. With almost feverish haste he fumbled for the stirrup, stepped astride. Gun ready, then, he kneed the dun and sent it picking a slow and cautious course, slanting toward the street. They came down between a couple of log buildings, and here Clausen

136

reined in a moment to stand in the stirrups while he swung a cautious glance in both directions.

He was in luck. With the searchers drawn off by a false alarm the section of the street before him lay deserted, except for a small clot of men standing in front of the Dutchman's—men who were apparently taking no part in the hunt but had been drawn outside by curiosity. They were all that stood in his way, and they did not worry him much.

He pulled his horse to the left and eased at a slow walk down the street toward them, holding the dun to the shadows, gunbarrel lying along his left thigh. A tense moment passed, as the distance narrowed between him and that group at the saloon. Watching them, he saw how one suddenly bent forward as though to take a closer look; he was prepared for the yell when all at once it came: "Who's that coming? Hell—*ain't that Clausen?*"

Instantly Virg Clausen booted the dun and the revolver swung up and drove two shots, as quick as he could trigger. He did not expect to make a hit; but, as he had hoped his bullets demoralized and split them, amid a racket of startled yells.

The dun, its hoofs lifting dollops of mud and meltwater, bore down at a gallop on the saloon and past it. Beyond stood the hotel and the livery barn and a few more buildings—and after that, he would be in the clear with nothing at all to stop him.

It was then that he saw the man who had walked down the hotel steps and alone into the street.

Whoever it was he stood bareheaded, leaning on a walking stick, a revolver in his right hand. As Clausen pounded nearer, a glimmer of window light showed the faint gleam of thinning, grayish hair; he recognized the face of Sam White turned toward him, waiting. A grunt of surprise broke from him, his mouth hardened, and he fired.

Unlike those others at the saloon, Sam White did not panic or even appear to flinch. Instead he tossed aside the walking stick and, standing on braced legs, brought up his revolver in both hands. Clausen could not swerve; on one side was the scattered line of buildings, on the other the

137

deep ditch carrying its swirling torrent. He had no choice but to run the old man down.

Swearing, he fired again. The lone figure held its position, straight in the path of the pounding horse. Clausen looked into his face, and into the muzzle of the gun held in front of the old man at arm's length and took deliberate aim. Then, almost under the horse's nose, the gun exploded in a blossom of searing flame.

A massive weight struck Virg Clausen in the center of his body and drove him from the saddle. It was only his insensate and lifeless body that struck the sodden ground.

CHAPTER XV

On approaching Morgantown from the valley by night, one saw its lights as an oddly twisted serpentine sprawl threading the tilted throat of the gulch. Jim Bannister pulled rein a moment to consider those lights, and afterward lifted his glance toward Claude Youngdahl's fine house perched high above the town's ugliness.

He wondered if the banker was up there now, perhaps waiting for a report from Gil Rickman concerning the outcome of tonight's mission to Tepee. He felt an urge to go up there himself and tell Youngdahl his scheme for eliminating Grady Sullivan had failed. But he shrugged the thought away.

The banker was no concern of his. Youngdahl would be hearing the news soon enough, if he had not already heard it. It might actually be pleasant to be there and watch the man's face when he was told, see if there was anything that could really shake the man's complacency; but he doubted Youngdahl was ready yet to admit defeat.

Today very little had been settled in the valley, even though this particular play for power had been turned back. All the same, Bannister could not see Youngdahl as a real menace—not for very long. He was not forgetting the scene

138

with Irene Youngdahl in his hotel room. The banker might be a cunning man, but in his wife he had met his match. One of these days Irene was apt to find the man she was looking for; and when she did, Claude Youngdahl's days would be numbered.

Well, that was a situation that would work itself out. Whatever happened, it would probably be to Morgan Valley's benefit. . . .

Early as it was, he noticed in passing that the windows of Sam White's shack were dark, and judged that Sam must already be asleep. He pushed on, debating whether to stop at the jail for Bert Dakins or look into the matter of Virg Clausen without bothering with Morgantown's new marshal.

It was at that moment, without warning, that a familiar voice suddenly called his name in a breathy exclamation: *"Jim! Jim!"*

He pulled in sharply as Stella Habord appeared at his horse's shoulder, clutching her threadbare coat about her with one hand while the other caught at his bridle. "Don't go into town!" she cried with an urgency that brought him, quickly puzzled and alarmed, down from the saddle.

"What is it, Stella?" he demanded. And added, before she could speak, "Look! I've got business that won't wait. I have to find that fellow, Clausen. . . ."

"Clausen is dead. Sam killed him."

That staggered him and made him blind. *"Sam?"*

Stella had ahold of his sleeve and was shaking his arm. "Jim, you have got to get away! You don't know what just happened!" An anxious look across her shoulder, into the darkness, and then she said urgently, "Hurry! Come up to the house. Tie your horse where it won't be seen. . . ."

Baffled, he hesitated; then said, "All right," knowing it was not a time to doubt her judgment.

When he had climbed the steps and, after a careful look around, slipped into the shack, all the shades had been drawn. A glance into the bedroom showed that Sam was not there; the two of them were alone.

Bannister went into the kitchen where he found Stella

working with concentrated quickness, ransacking pantry shelves and cupboards for tinned goods and other things which she piled on the kitchen table. To his astonishment, he realized that she was busy assembling a pack. In the lamplight her face was white, and he detected a shine of wetness on her cheeks.

"Will you tell me what this is all about?" he asked her gently. "And what did you say about Virg Clausen?"

She answered briefly, as she worked. "He was caught trying to rob the bank. When Will Farley wouldn't open the safe Clausen shot him, but Will lived long enough to identify him. There was a manhunt; Bert Dakins nearly went to pieces, running around like a chicken with its head off."

"But, Sam—what was he even doing out of bed?"

"I don't know. I haven't been home most of the day. Apparently, while I was out, he got up and dressed and walked up into town—and somehow he ran into Clausen. I heard Clausen tried to run him down, but Sam stood firm and shot him right out of the saddle.

"Suddenly, he's a hero. Henry Barnhouse was telling me he thinks the council will reconsider its decision to fire him. Isn't that wonderful, Jim?"

"Yes," Bannister agreed, though he was as baffled as ever. "I've felt all along that what Sam needed was some kind of a shove to get him out of that bed and on his feet. And then a chance to prove to himself, and to the rest of the town, that he's as good a man as he was six months ago. But, Stella. . . ." He stepped to take her by the shoulders, force her to turn and face him. "You haven't explained—this." He nodded at the things on the table, the pack she had been hurriedly assembling as she talked.

Slowly her face lifted, and now he saw the definite mark of tears on her cheeks. "We knew it had to come, Jim. But not so soon!"

"You mean—?"

"I mean, the word is out about you! A couple of riders left this morning to test the pass road; and up beyond Squaw Head they ran into a freight outfit that was trying to be first into the valley with supplies. The wagon may need another day or more to make it in, but the crew was full of gossip.

And the big piece of news was about you having been seen last year, over around Antelope and in the Downey-Cabra Springs country. It's assumed you must still be in this part of Colorado. They had a good description—"

Bannister finished, grimly, "—and our friends realized they'd had a twelve-thousand-dollar reward living in their midst all winter, and they turned around and rode back to spread the word."

She nodded. "They only got in a few minutes ago. They still don't know for certain you're the man, but the town's suspicious enough to hold you until they can investigate. And you could have walked right into them!"

"Well, I didn't. One more thing I have to thank *you* for. . . ."

Stella picked up the pack she had put together, thrust it at him. "Jim, you have to go! Here's food enough for a few days, at least. Do you need a fresh horse?"

"The bay will do." Suddenly, like a weight settling upon his shoulders, he felt the real meaning of this. It was a moment he had known must come, and he had tried to prepare himself. But now, resuming the life of a hunted man was all the more bitter for what he would leave behind. Looking at the woman, he swallowed and to cover his feelings said gruffly, "I'd better be moving—before they think to come here looking for me."

"Let me check, first."

In the living room he blew the lamp, while she tried the door to test the darkness outside for danger. It seemed quiet enough, and they swiftly went out and down the steps to where Bannister had tied his horse in a bay of rock and brush.

He lashed the pack of supplies to his saddle and turned, then, sobered by the moment. Bareheaded, she lifted her face to his in the dim starlight. "Stella—"

"I'd still go with you," she said quietly. "You only have to say the word."

"I know. But it's a word I won't let myself say. . . ." She came against him suddenly, her arms reaching for him. He kissed her, tasted the salt of tears, and laid his cheek against her hair. "There really isn't much to say, is there?" he said bleakly, and heard a single sobbing catch of breath; after that she pulled away again.

"Remember that I'll be waiting," she told him. "If you ever need me—if you can find some way to get word—"

"We'll see."

And then he stiffened, turned quickly at the startling sound of a bootsole crunching gravel. The shape of a man loomed against the brush; Bannister's hand slapped at the skirt of his coat, to clear holster leather, then fell away empty—not because he saw the glint of starlight on a drawn gunbarrel but because, in that instant, he recognized the man who held it. "Sam!" he exclaimed. "This is Jim Bannister. . . ."

"Yes!" The lawman's voice sounded odd; he made no move to lower the gun. "Didn't expect to see me on my feet, did you?"

"Stella's told me what happened this evening—and that you may get your job back. I'm glad to hear that."

"Are you?"

Something was definitely wrong; he knew it then. Silent and frowning, he looked at the older man and at the dim reflection of the gunbarrel.

"I've already killed one murdering skunk this evening," Sam White declared. "It'd really be something to top it by bringing in the most wanted outlaw in the Rockies!"

Stunned, Bannister thought he understood. "That would make it up to the town, I guess, for being taken in and forcing them to pin a deputy's star on me."

"Oh—that!" the old man said roughly. "The town ain't holding that against me. Sid Noon himself told me he reckoned anyone could make a mistake. . . ."

"Then, *why*, Sam?" Stella demanded, hurt and bewilderment in her voice. "Surely not for the twelve thousand! I don't believe, for a minute that a thing like that could turn you against a friend!"

"You think I'd touch the money?" the lawman cried, stung. He broke off; when he spoke again his voice was quiet, but it trembled with emotion. "Just don't talk to me of friendship—not after this man worked behind my back

142

when I couldn't defend myself. Not after he took my help and then tried to steal my job!"

Bannister said crisply, "Sam, that's not true!"

"You deny it?"

"Of course he denies it!" Stella exclaimed, unable to stay silent. "Whatever would give you such a notion?"

"Hell, I got a witness! Mrs. Youngdahl herself told me what she heard during a council meeting in her own living room."

"Irene Youngdahl! You'd believe *her*?"

"I also went to Lloyd Canby," Sam went on stubbornly. "He admitted the truth of it. He said there was actually talk between Bannister and the council of kicking me out and putting him in the job permanent."

"Oh, Sam!" Stella tried to take his arm but he shook her off, the gun in his grasp unwavering. "You must not have understood! *I've* been talking to Canby, too, and to Henry Barnhouse. Go back and check with them again—because, they both told me Jim was offered the marshal's post and refused it. Do you hear me? *Refused* it, Sam—on *your* account. He threw away the advantage Youngdahl's backing might have given him!"

Bannister moved his shoulders in an angry shrug, "Let it go, Stella," he said tiredly; and to the old lawman: "I won't draw on you, Sam. Not after all that you've done. But you won't take me alive, either. You'll have to pull that trigger, so you might as well do it now."

The breath left Sam in an audible sigh. "Oh, hell," he grunted, and stabbed the gun into its holster. "I might of known I had it all wrong. . . . But you better not waste any more time talking, Jim. Stella's told you what's been happening?"

"She told me," Bannister said. "I'm ready to travel."

He turned and found the stirrup, rose and settled into leather, already feeling the pull of the trail drawing him on. Sam stepped close, placed a hand on his knee. "You know how to strike the pass road. I doubt there'll be anyone after you tonight. You should be able to make good distance before you camp. There's a freight outfit in the timber, a dozen miles beyond the Squaw's Head—go easy when you ride-around them. After that, you should be all right."

Bannister nodded. "I think I've got the picture."

Stella was on the other side of him, then. He leaned, swept an arm about her shoulders, drew her to him. Their lips met and he felt hers tremble and then firm. It was as hard a thing as he had ever done—to let her go. He straightened in the saddle, took the reins. The bay moved restlessly under him.

"So long for now," he said softly, and kneed the horse into motion.

For long minutes the old man and the young woman stood together, listening, even when the darkness of the lower gulch swallowed him up.

Presently Sam White stirred himself, turned his head and looked at the lights of Morgantown strung out along the twisted gulch. He spoke into a brooding quiet.

"That there is a man, Stella. But I reckon we won't be seeing him again."

"I won't believe that, Sam," she answered quietly. "I won't let myself believe it."

He peered sharply at the dim oval of the face beside him; in suddenly dawning understanding he nodded. "You go right ahead believing what you have to, girl," he told her gruffly. "Maybe there's nothing else makes any sense, in this dimwitted world. . . ."

144